TIDES

SARA FREEMAN

GRANTA

Granta Publications, 12 Addison Avenue, London W11 4QR

First published in Great Britain by Granta Books in 2022
This paperback edition published by Granta Books in 2023

Originally published in the United States in 2022 by Grove Press, New York

A CIP catalogue record for this book is available from the British Library.
1 3 5 7 9 10 8 6 4 2

ISBN 978 1 78378 7593
eISBN 978 1 78378 760 9

Offset by Avon DataSet Ltd, Alcester, Warwickshire
Printed and bound by CPI Group (UK) Ltd, Croydon, CR0 4YY

www.granta.com

For Jeff

On the long bus journey out, she doesn't cry or even have a single thought that she can name. She watches the dark impossibility of the road instead, the mostly empty seats ahead of her, the head of a woman a few rows up, listing forward and then jolting back. She does not sleep. She wants to be awake to make her declaration at the border. She will show her passport and when they ask, *Where to?* she will say without hesitation, *The sea.*

She does not have to leave. No one says: *You must go*. No clothes thrown out the window, no eviction notice. Her husband is already gone by then; she was the one to tell him that he had to go. She could say it was the baby—her brother's and his wife's. His sweet squawking through the open window in the apartment beneath hers. She could no longer live in this fixed way: their joy so firmly lodged beneath her grief. She could say that.

(

The motel advertises an ocean breeze but is nowhere near the beach. She waits in the small room, for something, for someone. She has turned her phone off, but she still feels it in her palm, waiting to bleat back to life. To deliver what message? *I love you. I miss you. Come back.* She left a note for her brother and his wife. No explanation or apology. *I'll be fine!* That's what she wrote. She asks at the reception desk about another motel, nearer the water this time. The woman behind the counter has eyebrows like tadpoles swimming lazily across her forehead. She says there is a town she might like, remote, for rich folks mostly, about thirty miles up the coast. There is a hostel there too. She puts her index finger on a map, her nail filed down to a tidy point. This one is canary yellow, the surrounding ones sky blue.

She gets a ride from a man who is delivering ice across the state. His eyes are blue and inflamed, his hands raw and meaty. The town sign reads: *This Road Leads to Rome*, with an ugly drawing of the Colosseum, followed by the population, 2,353. When she gets out in the town's central square, she touches the hard shell of the truck with gratitude and it is so cold, the hairs on her arm stand up.

(

There is no coliseum in this Rome. Instead, a supermarket, a Greek restaurant, an Italian restaurant, a seafood spot, an ice cream shop, a wine store, a laundromat, a pub, an inn, a garden center, a health center, a hardware store, a library, a clothing store, a pharmacy, a marina, and a dump.

The sea, in this new town, is surprisingly hard to get to. It is somehow everywhere and nowhere. She needs an invitation, a private viewing: through the stately homes, and onto the other side, where everything is vast and pristine. The other her, the one she left behind, would have easily slid between the giant piles, past the outdoor furniture, past the slim lounging bodies and their pure-bred dogs. Everything belonged to her then; that was back when she believed that nothing that could so easily be had wasn't somehow already hers.

《

From her bedroom window in the hostel, she can see it best: the sea and its expanse, edging in and then pulling back. She doesn't want to be in it yet. It is warm out, but she still feels frozen, blood-let, fleshless. She is content, for now, to watch the comings and goings from afar.

In the evenings, she walks along the town's main drag. It is shaped like a horseshoe. She often sees the same faces twice, on their way to the ice cream store, and then on their way back. There are often tears on the return journey, mostly children's, but on one occasion a grown woman's and her wife's. Once desire is met, she thinks, there is only turning back from it. There is not much to do or see in the town at night: just tourists dining al fresco, prodding swordfish slabs and slurping oysters. A busker nearby crooning, *Oh, oh, Mexico*, as if he might be in this town in error. The first nights, she stops and finds a place among the small crowd gathered before him. But one evening, mid-song, he looks up and greets her with a complicit nod. Now, when she hears the busker's familiar sound, she passes by without so much as looking up.

She asks around at the hostel, and they tell her she is right: the prettiest beaches are cut off by the houses. It wasn't always like this, they say, the coastline so private and all. Some of the richest families used to turn a blind eye, but not anymore. In a few weeks, once the season is over, then that's a whole different story. For now there's the public beach, of course, but that's nothing to write home about. That's good, because she's not planning to write home about anything. They laugh, hearing her say this, and she thinks for a moment that nothing much has changed: she can say a few words in the right order and get people to love her for a moment.

(

She finds it, flanked by the supermarket and the garden center: a slip of public sand. There is an orange tent set up at the far end of the beach and two pairs of swollen, mangled feet sticking out. When she walks by, the screen is zipped halfway down, so that she can't see any faces, she can only hear the syncopated sound of their snoring.

She wonders what she will do when the money runs out. The thought is sticky, the first one like this, insisting on its own importance. It seems absurd somehow, that she must think of it, make something of this thought. The beach ends and there is a large expanse of dark, jagged rocks. She walks across the fraught ground, canvas shoes sliding dangerously beneath her. She slips and catches herself then slips again and falls hard on the rock. Not pain, just the feeling of everything coming up from within. She sits there, looking around, for someone, a witness to her fall, a hand to grip as she steadies herself back up. But there is no one, just the dome of orange light tented in the distance.

(

She buys a large lemonade filled with crushed ice and drinks it until her teeth and brain are numb. She shuts her eyes hard and when she opens them again, she is surprised to find that everything is still there: the lemonade truck, a few waves quietly churning in the distance, the sand, dank and gray, waiting to be touched.

She wakes one morning, clutching her stomach. No time has passed; her husband is by her side. He touches her rounded stomach with his palm. *Nearly there*, he says, speaking into her belly button. She is awake now, her palm on her own skin, the fingers cold and thin. Her belly is nearly concave, more than empty. She has been gone for three days, maybe four, or maybe it is six, and since then she has eaten a sleeve of saltines, some peanut butter from a spoon, a few beers, a lemonade, some fries, and some licorice. She is saving money; she doesn't have much left. One thousand seven hundred and thirty-three. If she needs more, she'll turn the phone on, write her brother a message. He has never said no to her before. His only sister. She'll write to him and say something like this: *I am changing.* Or better yet: *I have changed.*

《

She sees children everywhere, in the flesh, but also in what they leave behind: striped swimsuits hanging over banisters and beach chairs, colorful pails discarded on the beach. When she sees them, children and their traces, she turns her head away. It is her head that does the turning. She speaks, as though defending herself before a jury: *This* is not about *that*.

At the town's small marina, day-trippers clump around the seafood spot, composing their seaside shots: plush pink lobster rolls, heaped French fries snapped from above. In the background, a row of handsome wooden yachts, sterns wagging; a fisherman, sun-creased and smoking, unloading his mid-August catch. She doesn't stay long; the smell here makes her queasy. Fish entrails and sunscreen, cooking oil reused one time too many.

〈

In a shop window along the main drag, she spots a letterpress sign: *Keep Rome Off the Map*. In this town, the patrician crowd don their modesty like a crown: beat-up station wagons, worn-in khakis, styles from thirty years past.

The diner here is famous for its 1950s memorabilia. She sits at the counter and orders the lumberjack special. She pictures a lumberjack laying her across his lap, breaking her, like a twig, in half. She eats a sausage link and one of three sunny-side-up eggs, a bit of the pancake just for the mouthful of syrup. This diner, with its defunct Coke machines and jukeboxes and old graphic lunch boxes, reminds her of her mother's house, crammed with dangerous nostalgia. A woman and her toddler sit nearby. She spoons cereal into his wet little mouth. He dribbles and she wipes. He dribbles and she wipes. Easy as that. The woman is wearing all linen and a large-brimmed hat; she looks old to be a mother. But who is she to say who is old and who is not? She was thirty-five when she got pregnant, thirty-six when she lost her child. And now she feels one hundred, or maybe only seven years old. She looks a moment too long. Something passes between them, the mother and her, a warm current of it: pity, or maybe its cousin, contempt. When she asks for the bill, the man at the counter, pointing to the table where the mother and son were sitting, says, *They said to say good luck.*

In the bathroom mirror, she lets herself look up. She sees what the woman must have seen: the gaunt face, the hair matted to one side, the lips chapped, the nails bitten to the quick. She splashes cold water on her face and pulls her hair back. She looks nearly dead. *This* is not *that*. She looks down at her clothes; they are dirty but intact.

It is hot. The hottest day yet. August, slinking into September. Still hot by the evening, when the sun is a red face dipping its chin into the water. The public beach is empty. Everyone is on their patios sipping Campari and eating pistachios, saying their farewells. She removes her canvas shoes, her jeans and shirt, and moves into the water—sharp and cold as a knife's edge. She swims out until, when she turns her head, she can no longer make out her clothes bundled up on the sand, just a single line of darkness in the background. The water is bitter now, the moon just a sliver in the night, barely any comfort at all. She is that sliver, she thinks, drowning in the dark. She could die here, so slight and sinking. Nothing but her body to buoy her up. Whatever reserves she had, she has lost them now. She feels a rush of heat around her, her own urine, terror at her own thoughts. She thrashes around, trying to turn back, but even this turning, this changing course, seems impossible: the body has forgotten how to lead. It takes an eternity to move against the current, the arms and legs dumb with disuse and then too much exertion. She kicks hard, and then softer, it is easier this way, without trying at all; she is moving forward and back, lulled by the waves. She is like this forever, until she hits something, a rock, and then her knees hit it too, and she finds that she can crawl. Beneath her, the hard, wet certainty of the ground. She manages to get to her feet, finds her clothes in their pile, falls asleep in a damp heap.

She wakes before the sun and sits up, stiff and cold. She has always wanted this: to slip beneath the surface, to dispossess herself. Now that she has done it, it is hard to remember how her self could have become such a bottomless pit: feed me, fuck me, fill me, love me.

❨

This is what it feels like to slip, she remembers telling her husband, when she was teaching him to ice-skate on the Ottawa Canal. *You can't teach someone how to slip.* He was right: you slip and then you've slipped and so you know.

Sometimes, she pictures them: her brother and his wife, discussing her now that she is gone. *Impossible*, that's what they would say. Or maybe, instead, *beyond repair*.

〈

The management has moved her things. *You were gone for two nights*, they tell her. She can remember only one, but she doesn't want to fight. Her things include: a toothbrush, a sweater, two T-shirts, one pair of jeans, the biography of a famous chef, all stuffed inside an old backpack with her brother's initials embroidered on it: *P.S.T.* They have placed her in the large dormitory. She can tell from the work boots neatly lining the beds that the place is full of men. She buys a six-pack of beer and some cigarettes and brings them with her to the beach. She will wait until the men are sleeping before climbing back into her cot. She lies down. The beer and cigarettes are effective; she feels herself drifting pleasantly into the night. Today she has only eaten half a packet of tea cookies and a banana. The waves are loud, brimming over, coursing to their violent meter. Before she falls asleep, she thinks: This is what babies must hear when they are held inside the womb.

She wakes to a hand on her shoulder, a gruff one, a man's hand, shaking her awake. A light so bright she can't make a thing out, only voices, two of them, ordering her to stand up. She is on the beach, her hand clutching at wet sand. Her eyes adjust and she sees them: two men in uniform. Father figures, she thinks. She smiles up at them. They don't smile back. Bad daddies. She says something out loud, but it sounds more garbled than what she had in her head. They grab her, one arm and then the other, not at the armpit, but by the wrists, as though she were just a kid. Swing me around and around and around and around. But it hurts, the joints are no longer loose; they are fixed in place. *You're hurting me*, she says, this time clearly. *I'm not doing anything wrong.* They point to the empty beer cans, more of them than she can remember drinking. She tries to explain: there were men in the hostel, she was just waiting for them to fall asleep. She is sitting in the back seat of their car now, hands cuffed. They have forgotten to put her seatbelt on. The metal beneath the seat hits her tailbone, a familiar, pummeling beat. She has never been this cold, this brittle, her entire body caught up in a single spasm. *I'm still scared*, she says, at the door of the hostel: a giant mouth, gaping open. She begs the fat officer to take her inside, sit with her until she falls asleep, but he tells her, *Grow up, lady*, and takes his leave. Inside, all the men are sleeping, quiet as babies. She falls asleep quickly. When she wakes, she looks around and all the men are already gone.

15

The men are here for the season: blueberries, raspberries, blackberries. Three of them are working on a house. *The house is so big*, she hears one of them say in Spanish, *you could fit my whole village inside of it.*

«

They are kind, concerned for her. They say, *Güera, que pasó?* pointing to her clothes, her shoes. She tells them, *Nada*, nothing has happened. They let her in on their talk. She likes being near them; she understands one in five words, this is enough.

She is like a ball being passed from one set of hands to another, none of them holding on for too long. In the communal kitchen, one offers her tortillas with beans, the other spaghetti from a can; another gives her cookies mortared with jam and cream. In the mornings, she wakes with them before dawn. They eat white bread slick with margarine, and make her Nescafé their special way: they heat the milk and let the granules dissolve, then add three heaping spoonfuls of sugar. The older one says: *Mija, tienes que comer*, and makes her eat a second piece of Wonder Bread sloppy with supermarket jelly.

One evening, she sees a few of the men huddled around the kitchen table, hunched over the cracked screen of a phone. In miniature, she makes out a penis sliding between two breasts as taut and playful as helium balloons. They turn the screen off as soon as they see her. They disperse, scatter back into the dormitory.

(

The young one asks her: *Cómo te llamas?* She tells him without much thought: *Nada*. She likes it as a name, *Nada*. The girls who work at the reception desk think it's strange: how much time she spends with the men, sitting and biting her nails, not talking at all. One morning, she finds her few clothes at the foot of her bed, folded and washed.

Sometimes, in the evenings, they watch a movie on the small television hanging from the ceiling. They all have to crane their necks to see the tiny men on the screen dangling from helicopters and saving women from burning buildings. Sometimes when she gets bored by the action, she walks around and picks up their empty beer cans, rinses them, arranges them neatly by the bin.

《

For the first time in her life, she does not dream.

In the middle of the night, she hears the young one in his bed. His moans are so low and muffled, she feels as though they are coming from her, a rush of blood in her own veins, a throbbing at her own throat. Not so long ago, she might have slipped out of bed, slid her hand between his legs, and told him: *Let's try this instead.* The sound makes way for another, not sex but slow, withheld sobs, those of a much littler boy. Her body is stiff with remorse. She has no rounded edges anymore, no warmth to proffer him.

(

In the morning, she finds it hard to look at him. She pours him his cereal instead, his milk, dunks a spoon in it. *Aqui tienes.* He boasts about a girlfriend, a toddler back home. Two years, six months, three weeks, and a day: this is how long it's been since he's seen them last. He is thick and strong and still growing, his front teeth too big for his mouth. She wants to touch the down on the upper lip and say, *There, there.*

She counts backward, tries to do her own dismal math. August, July, June, May, April, March. Five months since she saw her own child, eyes stuck shut, limp as an unclenched fist.

☾

James Taylor is gone, but Joan Baez is there to replace him. She sings a song called *Colorado,* in which the only lyric is *Colorado*, repeated over and then over again. When she thinks the song is over, Joan begins again: *Colorado . . . Colorado.* In Canada, where she is from, no one ever sings songs about Alberta.

The season is nearly done. She lets the fact of it wash over her. The city folks have gone home, the hostel will close. She hears it but the words are water and she a gripless surface, a flat expanse. The day arrives and the men are all packed up. *I miss you*, she tells them in Spanish. She doesn't know the future tense for *missing*. There is a van here to pick them up. She stands outside, nose running, waving, a single arm wrapped around her for warmth, a mother sending her boys off on the school bus.

❨

The girls at the reception desk tell her she's got one day to clear out. They feel sorry for her, but they are only teenagers. *Senior year*, they say to her like a question and an answer all rolled into one. She tries to turn her phone back on, but the screen stays dark, every crevice filled with sand.

They tell her that if she helps them clean the place, she can stay three more nights. She vacuums and mops the floors, cleans the toilets and the scum between the tiles. She covers the furniture with tarps. She cleans the kitchen, consolidates all the half-eaten boxes of spaghetti into a single Ziploc bag. In the lost and found, she finds three dresses and two sarongs, a hot plate and a night-light, an elegant fountain pen with the two parts of the nib violently split apart. The three of them collect 168 dollars' worth of coins, under the beds, inside the couches, in the laundry room under the machines. The girls whisper to one another and sheepishly offer her twenty dollars in dimes. She finds a lighter with a woman's silhouette on it. When it is upright, the woman wears a pretty pink dress. When she flips it upside down, the woman bares her ample breasts, a tassel, mid-twirl, on each nipple. During their lunch break, she sits in the sun and flips the lighter up and then down, up and then down again. The girls place a paper plate at her feet, a hot dog adorned with two perfect stripes: one red, one gold.

《

Three hundred and twenty-three dollars. This is counting the twenty dollars in dimes.

The three days are up. *Just one more night*, she begs. The girls hesitate, convene privately. *Fine*, they say, *but tomorrow morning you're gone, or else we're going to have to call the boss*. The next afternoon, they find her, still asleep in the cavernous room. *He's coming now*, they warn her. *He knows about you and he is displeased*. They use this word, *displeased*, as though it is a word she might not have heard before. They lay it on thick. They took a chance on her and now she's going to have to pay. She was their age once, sharpening herself against her own blunt force. And so she tells them she's very sorry, gives them fifty dollars, and buys them a six-pack each before taking her leave.

☾

There are just hours left before sundown. Her backpack is heavy with hostel gleanings; the weight bears down on her shoulders, right down into her heels. Maybe she'll sleep on the public beach; she thinks of the tent, the mangled feet. She buys an ice cream cone, soft vanilla sprinkled with a messy hand. She walks along the main street, not thinking, every mouthful too sweet. She takes inventory of her skills. The list is short and so, easy to remember.

That evening in the pharmacy, she buys soap, razors, shampoo, and a bottle of cheap perfume. Mascara in a bright pink tube, a plum-red lipstick, foundation one grade of beige too dark—every item the cheapest she can find. She pays twenty dollars for a day pass at the health club. She asks how much for just a shower. *There's no price for that, miss.* She washes her hair, once, twice, three times, each strand stiffened with salt and grease. She looks down from time to time. She doesn't recognize the body beneath: feral, bleak. She shaves everything off. She forgot to ask for a towel so she walks around naked, drying herself off. She clips her nails and plucks her eyebrows, brushes her teeth. Two women in their sixties walk past her, catch a glimpse; she is denuded, goose-bumped, a chicken with her feathers just off. They stare down sheepishly at her feet. She slips on one of the dresses from the hostel's lost and found. Floral, cheap. She is tall, and this spaghetti-strapped shift is for someone shorter; it hits too high on her thighs. In the mirror, she sees what she will look like to others: she is not displeased. Only she knows what is amiss, like a loose tooth at the back of her mouth holding on by just a few threads. From time to time, she touches the fact of it with her tongue.

He is easy enough to spot. He orders a beer before the last one is halfway done. Rich boy, she thinks, hair smoothed back, gold pinky ring nestled in flesh. Prep school, financier, end-of-season loaf. She sits next to him. His teeth are small, his gums inflamed. He is already gone, left the building. She doesn't want money, she tells him, just a house to hole up in, a bed for the night. She takes his hand; she feels the fat pooling at the knuckles. She wonders if he ever takes the ring off, if he can. No, she doesn't do drugs, not that kind. *It's a real problem around here*, he says, in his newscaster's drone.

(

He is not a bad guy, she thinks, just a dummy, a clown. The ice clanks against his teeth, the cold sinks through her. She asks him to take his blazer off, to let her wear it. She is chilled to the bone, she tells him, dying of cold. He takes his wallet out of the inside pocket, flips it open. Now, he'll show her his sweetheart, she thinks. But he takes out his own college ID and points to the picture: *I want you to see what I looked like when I was sober.* In the photograph, he is good-looking, slim-faced, jaw pressed proudly out. Now there is one large fold of fat in which his face is propped up. She takes his hand and places it on her lap. She doesn't mind. This is the easy stuff.

She was the one who taught herself to read. *B* and *A* makes *BA*. Everyone asked her, incredulous, *How did you do that?*

༄

He lists back and falls off his stool, takes her with him. She is lying above him: flotation device, emergency raft. It takes a long time for the patrons to turn their heads, to witness the wreckage. She gets off him and pulls at his hand, but he is heavy, dead weight at the bottom of a slippery rope. *He's bleeding*, she says, and three big men come to hoist him up.

Such a pretty house, she says, despite herself. It's his parents' house. Large enough so he can lumber up the back stairs without waking them up, a house designed around its blind spots. She remembers a talk she attended when she was in her early twenties. The architecture of estrangement. She had liked the title, but the talk itself had been garbled, a series of simple words at the mercy of impossible sentences.

《

She doesn't know what she has in mind. One night, negotiated into two. She'll lie down, open up, the nib of a fountain pen split neatly apart. He has regained some strength. He looks over at her on the landing, has forgotten how he got here, who she is. He tells her she ought to go. But then, he lays his hand on her breast and says: *Fuck . . . well, fuck.*

In the room, there are two twin beds, which he insists on pushing together. *I'm a gentleman*, he informs her. *You had me fooled*, she says. She lies down, closes her eyes, falls into shallow sleep: She is in a wading pool, filling a red plastic cup with water and pouring it back out. Happy as a clam. She likes to watch the water moving with her, draining out over the lip of the plastic tub. *You taste so good*, he tells her, his mouth wet, a dog lapping water up from its bowl. Salt and sand and sea urchins, she thinks, and the vanilla crap she spritzed at the waistband of her undies. How did she know to do that? *B* and *A* is *BA*. Just like that. He crouches over her; she opens her mouth just wide enough to let him in. This is what he tastes like: dirty dog, pickled organs, ashtray, grout.

She wakes up, throat dry, head in her mouth. The two beds have slid slowly apart, the man crucified on one, she clammed inward on the other. The last thing she remembers is his slim dick prying open her mouth. She rolls onto her side: one leg down and then another. She is jelly, the room a spinning top. She finds her backpack, rummages through it, puts on her pants, a shirt that is clean enough. His wallet is on the ground; a ten and three ones. She leaves the ten and takes the ones, then takes the ten and leaves the ones. She could wait for him to wake up, big boy in his tiny bed. She could stroke his head, beg him for a few more nights. But *this* cannot be *that*, she thinks. She returns to the wallet, takes the university ID and slides it into her pocket. He should know better: there is no way back to the past.

It is early in the town. Earlier than she thought. The stores are shut, the air still cool from the night. The gulls sway and swerve. They land on the lips of garbage cans, tipping beaks into wide-open mouths. She would not say: I am hungry. She might say: I feel like a trash can emptied out.

❨

She used to say to her husband, if she can still call him that: *Not feeling is a feeling too.*

In the window of the wine store, there is a sign printed in red and black, falling a little to the right. *Help Wanted.* It reads like a confession, an act of desperation, poignant in its passivity. She sits on the picnic table out front, pulls her hair back, runs a moistened finger under each eye. She pinches her cheeks, her mother's trick. *Perks you right up!* She takes out a piece of gum. Her jaw works fast and hard, past the gum's chalky tongue, through to the bright flush of tropical fruit. How savage, she thinks, these rows of dueling teeth with that sleeping mound between them. She'd like to do something with her hands. She twists them around and around. She wants to move, to bend, to climb, to crawl. She waits; thoughts float by. She does not take the bait.

«

At noon, a man shows up, keys jangling on the side loop of his jeans. He is tall and hunched, and yet distinguished, handsome even. Middle Eastern or maybe Eastern European. He puts his hand through his dark, graying mane. Once, twice, three times. He opens the door, flips the sign on its front: *We're Open!* She waits awhile, spits the dead gum into her palm, makes the sign of the cross, *au nom du Père et du Fils et du Saint-Esprit*, leaves her backpack by the door, and walks right into the shop.

Yes, she tells him, she can sweep and wrap and shelve and count. She has spent fifteen years near the helm of such a ship. Three restaurants, two bars, and one nightclub. *That was an unfortunate interlude*, she tells him, *all those daylight hours down the drain*. She is impressed by her own performance. She sounds like the old self: dry, nearly self-possessed, cutting to the chase. *It's a temporary position*, he tells her, *until my wife gets back*. He'll pay her cash at the end of each week. *Good?* She nods. *Then, good*.

«

She walks three miles along the state road to the nearest motel. The honks of trucks feel almost celebratory, the aches from her falls nearly good company. The big white sign announces sixty-nine dollars for one night's sleep. She pays with her dimes and every bill she has left. She could use her credit card, but then she'd be a pin on a map, a woman hiding in plain sight.

She takes note: he did not mention how long his wife would be gone. *We'll burn that bridge when we get to it!* her husband used to say.

«

In room 8 of the highway motel, she sinks into the rough sheets. Her legs are cut up from the cheap razor, her pubis raw and welted. She puts her hand between her thighs, tries to rub sensation into the lifeless folds. But she doesn't feel a thing: just a little girl riding a bicycle on a flat, newly paved road, no mounting sensation, no imminent threat. On her left thigh, a bruise as big as a plum. She presses down on it, wants the splotch to expand—inkblot, Russia on a map. She sleeps with the television on, wakes to the sound of a couple locked in a pitiless fight: *I want my son!* the beautiful woman yells. *You can't have him!* the short man replies.

From the motel phone, she calls her brother. His wife is the one who picks up, her voice as high and unearthly as a child's. *We know it's you.* Every bit of life has been collectivized, their knowing too. Two skulls pressed together: two wills collapsed. *We're not angry. We understand. We get your grief.* Their baby in the background, giggling now, her brother cooing nearby. She catches a word of his nearer the phone—*lost*, or maybe it is *love*.

(

Just tell us that you're not dead, his wife is pleading; her brother is saying something too, his wife's voice strangling him out. She feels her own voice in her stomach, churning up sound. She rushes to the toilet and throws up her lunch: a bag of popcorn and two bottles of hard lemonade. When she gets back to the phone, the line is just a low hum.

When they were little—she a child and he an infant—they used to have to pry him out of her arms. She'd yell, cry, stomp. *He's my baby too.*

❨

She does not spend another day in the motel. *Laundry day*, she tells the boss on her first day of work, pointing to the overstuffed sack. *Good*, he says. *Good*. She wonders if *good* is his favorite word.

This is the cheese counter and this is the cheese wire and this is the scale and this is the wax paper and this is the twine. Here are the scissors; they're dull as a butter knife. These are the good wines and these are the less good wines. These are the whites and the reds and just the very best rosés. No, we don't do orange unless the person is famous or on their deathbed. These are from the Rhône Valley, and these are from the Loire. This is from a place in Sonoma. Have you been? No? Well, what can I say? These are from Spain and Portugal and these are from Italy. Between you and me, France for tradition, Italy for elegance, Spain for lunch. This one is from Morocco, French producer, it's exceptional. If someone asks, we don't do Malbecs. People are stubborn about their bad taste. This is the bathroom. If anyone asks, we don't have one. This is the storage room and then there's the attic for all the extra junk. I'll show you. Round the back and up the stairs. Be careful not to fall. Here is the key to that door. On second thought, you won't be needing the key to that door. Forget about that door. Forget about the key. This is the box cutter. And these are the boxes. You can start with those.

When he is in the storage room, she sticks the key into her back pocket. *You won't be needing that.* At the end of the day, he pushes a paper bag into her hands. Inside: an unsold brie sandwich, a bag of chips, three saltwater taffies. She walks by the ice cream store, now closed for the season, the bar where she no longer cares to be seen. The laundromat is open; she can stay there for a while. There is an attendant, an elderly man, reading a paperback on a white plastic chair. *Wrangled Heart*, the title reads. On the cover, a pale man with dark, lustrous hair, riding bare-chested on a horse. The old man doesn't look up from his book. Next to him a red Solo cup filled with coins. *Do you have change for a five?* He nods, still reading, a slow, old man's nod, and fishes the quarters out one by one, drops them into her cupped hands. He doesn't notice, or doesn't mention, that she hasn't given him a bill in exchange.

She waits until midnight before sneaking around the back. Up the steep outdoor staircase, right up to the door. The key clicks in the lock, a feeling like fate. The room is dark, a square of dispossessed land padded pink with insulation foam. A bare bulb, with a dangling cord she doesn't dare pull. She uses her lighter instead, the pretty lady on it smiling at her, urging her on. She is scared, every sound amplified, her chest throbbing in her neck. She can make out a wooden floor freshly painted, a toilet and a sink behind a beaded curtain, a few discarded chairs, a dozen wine crates lining the long wall at the back. She finds a stack of packing blankets huddled in the corner. She places them on the floor, opens the top fold and shimmies down until she is up to her ears in the dusty wrap. She does not sleep. She holds her breath; she shakes; she wills herself to breathe. There is a sound nearby, a tarp slapping against siding, a towel snapping at bare skin. She keeps her eyes sealed, her ears tucked inside the blanket's cocoon, until the morning light urges her to leave.

She puts the apron on, taps the roll of coins against the counter, breaks the paper, spirals it off, pulls two espresso shots, sweeps the front end of the shop, arranges the morning's delivery of pastries on a plate, tucks the mounds of ham between the bread's sharp flaps, carries the board out onto the windy sidewalk, flips it open, erases his unruly scrawl, replaces it with hers. This is a lot. She leans her entire weight against the counter, surveying her territory. In the display case, a wilderness of cheeses and cured meats. A customer comes in. *I'd like that one*, he insists, smudging the glass with his finger. She plunges her head into the cold case, digs around for a slab of Stilton right at the back. *Yeah, that one.* She breathes in the acrid cheese, punch in the face.

«

By noon, her stomach, an animal clawing at its cage. She wants to give it something smooth, uncomplicated: porridge served on a child's plastic spoon.

He walks around the store, massaging his neck with thick useful fingers, kneading flesh, dissolving tension, plotting his next task. *You look ill*, he tells her, *gaunt*, he says. *Don't move*. She waits, still as a wreath. He returns and hands her a cup of tea. *Take a break*, he says, not unkindly, pointing to the stool in the storage room. She sits on the low seat, limbs too long, an overgrown child waiting out her punishment. She slurps the milky offering, piping hot against the icy dam of her teeth.

That evening along the beach, the tent is gone, the lemonade truck too. She takes her shoes off, rolls her pants up, wades into the water. She looks out: no end in sight, the waves slow but stubborn in their returns. The air is balmy, a tease. A man in a bright green windbreaker walks a husky, fur in full bloom. The animal's eyes are wild searchlights, scanning the sand, dulled by the dim evening light. She settles where the sand meets the rock, empties her plastic bag, and presses it flat against the ground. She places on it two slivers of cheese, the hard ends of two baguettes, a nub of salami, waxy string dangling from its top. She takes a swig from the bottle of red left over from a mistaken case. *Plonk*, the boss told her, spitting it out into a cup. It tastes to her like metal, the inside of a sink. He wouldn't mind that she's taken these things, she thinks, softening the hard nub of bread in her palm. He is loose with his inventory, generous with his stock: in the afternoons, he gives away baguettes and pastries and opens, on a whim, bottles for customers to try and discuss. In fact, he isn't much like a boss at all. She eats in the dark. This is good. There is no surface on which her thoughts can find their footing.

Her second night in the attic room, she sleeps in fits and starts, swaddled, too hot inside the dusty packing blanket. This time, she doesn't slip out with the first sign of morning light. She decides she is no longer a trespasser, instead, a visitor, a guest with an absent-minded host. She sees it now clearly, in the halting morning light: a room with no clear purpose, a tentative patch of paint on the one finished wall, next to another, a little darker, a chromatic test. There are some paintbrushes, paint cans just bought, sticking out from a large carrier bag. She fingers the painted Moroccan tiles set up on the counter, only half-installed. The entire room is a tableau of will suspended, motivation stalled, effort put on pause. His wife's work, no doubt. She sweeps away the thought. She sets to work on erasing the signs of her own presence in the room. She stashes the backpack in an empty trunk; she moves the packing blankets back to their heap at the back of the room.

Everyone is very quiet in this shop, in this town, as though they are trying not to wake a child that has agreed, after a feeding, to finally go to sleep.

‹

I'd prefer you call me Simon, he tells her, *instead of boss*. She nearly laughs at the sound of his unsteady resolve, an actor prompted, after too much practice, to deliver his single line.

On her third night in the attic room, her terror returns, familiar interloper. Each noise is a morbid echo, a reminder of everything near and unknown. We are never alone, she thinks, sweating through her T-shirt, a damp chill grabbing at the bone, the sound of a flag flapping viciously outside the window. When she finally gets to sleep, she dreams for the first time in weeks. Surfaces in the dark: counters, tables, chairs, the waxy skin of a lemon, the smooth side of a large rock. In the dream, she touches blindly in the night: slick, impenetrable flatness. A light is switched on. Nothing is as it felt; every smoothness is scarred, pitted, diseased. Pumice stone, rain on snow, a dull green rot. She wakes up feverish, still sleepy, the false promise of a yawn gaping at the back of her throat.

In the morning, she washes above the small sink, behind the beaded curtain. She uses the corner of a T-shirt, a soft tongue lapping at her neck, at her armpits, at her pubis. The hairs down there are barbed, an unevenly tended crop. Her period has come. She stinks: nickel, barnyard, oxidized blood. During her shift the day before, she rolled up toilet paper into a tight coil, pushed it in like a cork. But overnight, she has bled straight through the paper and it has dissolved into a single clot. She pulls it out, this sopping wet rope, this dark surprise. Saturday, she'll get paid and she can go to the pharmacy, the health club to wash; but for now, the ocean is her only option.

((

She knows this cannot last, this sneaking in and out at dawn; she may get caught. And then what? She can think only in small measurements now: one minute followed by the next, an afternoon and then an evening.

The water is frigid, colder the further out she wades. Once the water is at waist height, she takes the underwear off, passes a rough hand under herself. A plume of blood suspended under her: watercolor, Rorschach blot. She sees: time standing still, a mobile static above a crib. She puts her underwear back on, splashes the blood out of her way, wades back to the shore. The beach is empty, seaweed strewn around like streamers torn down the day after a party.

《

She sweeps, she mops, she seeks out every errant crumb, every stuck fleck of cheese, every fingerprint, the dust settled on the tops of boxes and cans. Everything, she discovers, can and must be wiped. The day is overcast, and everyone has decided to stay home. Simon moves from the window to the storage room, back to the counter, as though he is waiting for a delivery, a visitor waylaid. His sigh is the longest, the most capacious she has ever heard. Maybe this is where she is stuck: inside a man's suspended breath, his hollowed-out chest. He sits on an overturned crate nearby reading his trade publication. He licks his index finger; he turns the page loudly, lets out a derisive snort.

On her break, she sits outside on the picnic table, smoking a Camel Light. She can't bear to sit on the low stool in the storage room, the smell of wet mop in her nose, the cleaning product's citrus edge at her throat. Two lean bodies move toward her, listing to the right. Their disorder is plain against the street's clean geometry—storefronts, sidewalks, benches, planters, awnings—cooperative, polite. Their clothes are surprisingly clean, their shoes pristine and white. But they disown them, their bodies disavow them: the woman's hoodie is unzipped, falling down past her shoulder, the man's pants sink low on the tiny waist, with no belt to hold them up. He lays his hand on the small curve of her ass. *Don't*, she screams, swatting him away. Her hair is pulled back, wet-looking, painted onto her scalp. Her face is muddled, as though someone has taken a hand across it and smudged it. She is seventeen or forty-seven or somewhere in between. She is the walking dead: the child inside her floating dangerously near the surface, gasping its final breath.

It happens very fast: the man grabs the woman, brings her close to him and growls, baring his teeth, looking savagely into her eyes. She tilts her head back, spits into his face; he shakes her, berates her: *You whore, you bitch, you twisted little cunt.* A grin and then her own growl, barking now, a rabid dog. She sets off, running, companion nipping at her tail, past the wine store, up where Main Street curves inward and then disappears.

《

She has seen her before, this woman. Not in the flesh, no, but conjured in her mind's eye, the dead end of a long, familiar road. On the way back into the shop, she meets her own reflection: the high forehead, the large gray eyes. She is glad to find it there, mostly unscathed, not the addict's face but her own.

For many years, she watched, with the fierce presentiment of the hypochondriac, for whatever was wrong in her to bloom.

《

Was someone slaughtering a goat out there? Simon's smile dances across his face. Behind the rosy curtain, a row of perfectly healthy teeth, a magic trick, *tada!* He is standing precariously on a ladder, trying to reach one of the far-away bottles. She sees him now, perhaps for the first time, as he really is: all limbs—feet and hands enormous and flat, his balancing on a ladder a feat of coordination, of proportion. His hair is unwashed, sticking out to one side; there is a witness missing from his life. And yet, beneath it all, something persistent, fat clinging to ribs, a good-natured boy, unerring in his loyalties. *They're probably from Inglewood*, he tells her, as if she will know what this means.

Later, when Simon is upstairs grabbing a case of Bordeaux, she returns to the street. She sees, against the litterless road, a dark mound on the sidewalk. She takes a few steps closer, a fleshy softness appears. Nearer still, she makes out a hoodie, the inside of the sweater splayed out, pockmarked, pilled. She picks it up, touches the stiff sleeves, a garment washed and dried on hot too many times. She brings it inside, stashes it under the counter among the stacks of old CDs, the clutter of binders and wires, tacky and disused.

«

Sometimes, she pictures it: her mother finding out that she is gone. *Selfish as a fox.* That's what she'll say. *Just like her father, leaves when the going gets tough.* She closes her eyes, shakes her head, waits for the flush of red against her eyes.

That evening, she sits inside the laundromat, waiting until it is dark and she can go back to her attic room. She tries to read a magazine. More compelling still: the forward motion of the machine's drum, spinning, catching, spinning again. This is intimate, she thinks, this wet commingling, the woman's sweatshirt mixed up amidst her things. She wonders, suddenly, what they have done with all her things, her room, the entire upstairs apartment. Her brother, she guesses, has been swift, impassive as he sifts through the ruins. Maybe he's rented a storage unit, cleared a cupboard, or at least a shelf. She can just picture it: her life stuffed haphazardly above his. He was like that as a child too, devoted to the appearance of order, a perfect room on the surface, but under the bed, inside the closets, everything in disarray, a mess only he could fathom. She'd have preferred it if he'd set everything to the curb: roadkill, deadweight, a bag of week-old bread.

On the way back from the laundromat, she feels fall's first chill and without much thought, she pulls the stranger's sweatshirt over her thin summer sweater. If you can't let go of *anything*, let go of *everything*. She read this once somewhere.

((

First thing Saturday, Simon hands her an envelope, no name, no mark of the pen. *Nada*, she thinks, remembering the men from the hostel. Three hundred seventy-five dollars per week. Enough to make ends meet. She's always liked this expression: *making ends meet*. She pictures it this way in her mind: the ends of a long rope coming together into a circle, a noose, maybe.

On her break that afternoon, she goes to the hardware store to make a copy of the attic key. The man behind the counter has a white beard that crawls past the far reaches of his cheeks. *What's this for, then?* he asks. She pretends not to hear, moves into the aisle instead. This one is for screws and nails and bolts and door handles. She takes a brass one into her hand, tries to turn it: soundless ratchet, useless toy. When she returns, the man hands her the key, its double. *You're working for Simon over there, aren't you? Poor fellow, what with the situation with his wife.* She lies, tells him she didn't know the boss was married. *Didn't even cross my mind to ask*, she adds, buoyed by her own pretense, her own play. *What's that expression? Don't shit where you eat?* the old man banters. She laughs, tells him he's right, she does like to keep things tidy. *You're a good girl, then*, he says. Let the old man think what he thinks. This is a familiar feeling: holding the truth and its opposite so near, tête-à-tête, a child dangling two dolls by the plastic scruff of the neck, orchestrating their animated talk. She walks out, both keys digging their teeth into her palm. She lets the small pleasure of her lie drop down, a penny at the bottom of a well.

On Sunday, her day off, she walks around: a loop, then back down again, a broader ellipse, and then one more time. Anything to escape the attic room, its dusty indeterminacy, its only purpose: for her to try, to fail, to sleep. The streets are dead, the summer crowd gone. Some of the houses, the ones nearest the water, are already boarded up. The old mansions up on the hill have their caretakers, seeding lawns, removing screens, painting trim. She prefers the town this way, she decides, mild-mannered, resting after its seasonal pillage. A regular heartbeat after a period of strain. She is a little like the town, letting up after a period of overuse: too much contact with other people, their chafing on her, her chafing on them. She passes by the church, hopeful for some warmth, even a hymn or two, a sermon to tune right out from, but even that appears to be closed for the season. She reads the sign out front, lacquered wood embossed with gold: *Here stands the hundred-year proof of unparalleled generosity and continued support of this town.* She recognizes the surname, *Endicott*. Brahmins, Mayflower types. She's seen or heard it before, in the shop, no doubt. On the right side of the sign, etched with a pocketknife: *Eloise loves cock.*

The library is closed, the health club shut. She'll need to wait somewhere until sundown before heading back up. The incident at the hardware store served as a reminder: she is a woman alone, everyone is taking note. The summer dwellers are no longer her insulation, her one-way mirror. She can no longer see without being seen. It is four, she guesses, nearly five. Only a few hours until the sun goes down and she can go upstairs, sit under her blankets, eat peanut butter from a spoon.

(

Inside the pub, there is a dying Sunday glow, a different crowd from when she was last here, all locals now, a couple drinking quietly, a group of elderly friends seated in a booth. They have identical haircuts: gray hair cropped short on top, left long at the back. The men look up at her and back down at their drinks, in quiet deference, to what? Long lives lived peacefully alongside their wives. The women fix their gazes on her, make their assessment; they do not nod or wave. At the bar, where she settles, a man is huddled in the corner, face red, his nose splayed out, torpedoed by too much drink. She has seen him before, in the early mornings, standing in the pub's doorway before the awning is out, smoking cigarettes, taking shelter from the wind, biding time before the first drop.

To her left, another man, younger, wholesome in contrast; she's seen him once before in the shop. He came in and bought two bottles of pinot grigio. *For the wife*, he said to her while paying, no wedding ring in sight. She orders a beer; he brings his stool nearer, his glass right up to meet hers. *Cheers.* He's got the handsome face of a high school dropout, his skin tanned from work outdoors, his hair nearly black and curtained down the middle. His eyes are hungry, a little bit dim. He loves his mother, she thinks, a little too much. *Cheers*, he says again, clanking her resting glass. She recognizes this innocence, this boyish insistence. This is her husband's breed of pup. She makes a mental note: I will not go to bed with him tonight.

(

There are still too many hours to fill before dark. Beer is the shortest distance between this and that point. She is sandwiched between the two of them: the old and the young, the drunk and the nearly drunk. She pictures herself this way: cold cut, melted cheese, a tomato slick with seeds.

It is dark now, the crowd thinned out to the dregs, the desperate bunch. *Don't pay attention to old Donaugh. He wouldn't hurt a fly.* The young one's arm is on her shoulder now; lead pipe, sandbag dragging her to the ocean floor. *You got a light, by the way?* She smells his breath: it is sweet, a little sickly, a baby's spit-up. She takes out the lighter, turns it upside down, shows him the trick. She is four beers in and hungry, although she doesn't know for what. *You just can't help yourself, can you?* Her brother used to say that, or maybe it was his wife. He is holding her hand now, their fingers are intertwined. *There is no wife, is there?* He shakes his head, smiles. *No, I just like how it sounds.*

Maybe they were right. That night, she moves with a fatalism that feels so familiar, no time has passed. The body works of its own accord, intent on spiting the mind and its resolve. She is nearly aroused. Then not at all. This is the desert of her mind: she is a parking lot, a strip of concrete just feet from the ocean. There is no turning back from oneself, she thinks, looking down into the stranger's slackened, happy face. He is searching for her, inviting her over to a lighter, sweeter place. He is not so bad, just a teenager given the keys to a car he doesn't know how to drive. He is guileless, an innocent; she is the liability, the snare. *You still here?* It's a matter of perspective, she thinks: she is near but also very far, a buoy being thrown back and forth just feet away from the shore.

〔

In the morning, he wants to talk, to stroke her hair, to turn her into someone he can love. *I've been waiting a long time for someone like you to come along*, he tells her. *I find that hard to believe*, she replies. He squeezes her thigh, tries to get her to look up into his eyes. *You know, a challenge, like.* She closes her eyes, moves her head a little side to side, tries to shake the idea of herself from his mind.

Aren't we lucky? her husband, Lucien, used to like to say, whenever he was doing something especially mundane, like pouring sour milk down the drain, or sticking his cold feet between her warm legs. Optimism with a whiff of defiance, a frisson of provocation.

❨

In the shop the next day, she moves from task to task with some of her old thoughtless ease. There is nothing in this job she cannot do. When she is done with her daily duties, she sets her mind to modest improvements. She rearranges the cheeses in the cheese counter: the sheep and goats to one side, the cows to the other. She writes out new signs for each one in her own tidy hand. *You did something*, Simon tells her in his half-sad, half-distracted manner. *Good*, he says. *Good*.

That night, as they are closing up the shop, there is a tap on the window, the sight of a delighted man's face grimacing outside. Every feature is animate, alive. Inside, he is immediately at home; he moves behind the counter, sweeps past her and straight to Simon, whom he kisses noisily on both cheeks. *I missed you, mein Schatz!* His is the loudest voice in this town. He has the keen excitability of a golden retriever: sniff, slurp, bark. *And who, might I ask, is this?* He moves in toward her, inspects her. *So tall, and those eyes! And that mouth, mein Gott, Bette Davis paying us a visit from the grave!* She forces a smile before excusing herself back to her task of covering the olives for the night. He follows her, a dog sniffing out a new rival at the pound. *Where are you living? And where are you from? I want to know everything!* She tells him, *A few miles outside of town, near the old quarry*, thinking of the dismal shack where she ended up last night. He doesn't look convinced. Simon breaks up their conversation with a bottle of Montepulciano. *I've got something for you to taste, Julian. I've been keeping this one for you.* The puppy paws at it. *Bravo! I'm not done with you yet, though, mademoiselle.* His look is invasive, and in a flash, dejected. Before he can pounce again, she moves to the storage room, slips her apron off, lets herself out the side door into the night.

Outside, in the cool, unfettered air, she catches her breath. She didn't know she'd been holding it. She is worn out, ready to go upstairs, to eat a granola bar in the dark, to sleep in fits and starts. But this stranger has unsettled her; he seemed set on turning her inside out. She doesn't know how long they will stay there, drinking and catching up. She has never seen Simon this way, entirely at ease, himself. She thinks of her bag upstairs stashed behind a crate. She is newly afraid for her things: the book she hasn't yet read, the few clothes she wears day in and day out, the phone, dead and yet still holding much of her old life. *I'm not done with you yet.* She walks through the alley into the streetlamp's depressed glow, follows the road that leads to the town's eastern edge. It doesn't take long to get to the mouth of the state road. She is walking quickly, but her mind is stuck, jogging in place, around the man's questions, his insistence, his suspicion. She feels herself drifting into the narrow lane, but she is too exhausted to steer herself back onto the shoulder. A car comes to a screeching halt. A window opens and a woman, her eyes bloodshot, is already yelling: *Have you gone insane? You're completely invisible, did you know that? That's really all I need tonight, your blood on my hands!*

In room 6 of the highway motel, she takes a long, hot bath, uses the small bar of cheaply scented soap to scrub the past two days off her skin. She is still shaking from the woman's outburst on the road. She washes her underwear in the sink, blows the hairdryer on it until the cheap material is dry and crisp. She finds the half-empty vending machine under a portico, buys some Bugles, a can of Diet Sprite. She eats, standing under the strip of fluorescent light. She takes a salty bite, flushes it down with a sweet sip. She looks for signs of life, but she is the only one here, just a truck hurtling by every few minutes, the sudden rumbling startling every time. In the room, she is too scared to turn the lights off, to surrender to sleep. She wonders if the woman who checked her in is still at the front desk or if she has gone home, wherever that is.

She wakes up feverish; the sheets are soaked through, her teeth clamped shut, her ears plugged up. Light steals through the bent edge of a blind. She manages to reach for her pants, the piece of paper, the phone number of the wine store. *Who is this?* Simon asks when he picks up. He sounds distant, hollow somehow. *Hello? Who is this?* She is still asleep, her jaw locked shut. She nearly forgets her own name. It is his name that comes up, air trapped inside a water cooler, bubbling up: *Paul.* Her brother's name instead of her own. *It's me. From the store*, she corrects herself. A long silence follows. *You're not quitting on me, are you?* She hears the stab of desperation in Simon's voice. *No, of course not. I just need a few days to get over this cold.*

«

This is my brother, Paul, she used to declare, whenever she could, as though she'd had some part in making him this way. Then she could be good by association, bright by proximity.

She spends the day in the borrowed bed, slipping in and out of sleep. She has forgotten something important: a word, a memory, a fact she has been asked to keep. She'll remember it soon. For now, sleep.

❨

There is a knock at the door. She is in her childhood bedroom. She doesn't want her mother to come in, to lift the blanket; she is naked underneath. *There's no need to yell, sweetie, it's me, Jean.* She sees her now: the woman from the front desk, a gray mop of hair flopped over her head. Jean has come armed with a vacuum cleaner, a neat stack of sheets. She is standing in the doorway, facing out, careful to maintain her guest's privacy. She'd like to say something like *Come in*, but her head is heavy, her mouth too dry, the skin of her lips tight and split right down the middle. A body moves through the room, hovering near, but she doesn't feel scared of it. It is so good to be amidst this woman's calm neutrality. There is a waterfall in the background; it is soothing, it lulls her back to sleep.

She feels a hand under her elbow, a gust of wind passing over her body. She is back on the beach, or maybe buried at sea. A voice like water inching over sand: *It's going to feel a little cool at first, but it'll bring the fever right down.* She doesn't know this voice, but she senses its goodwill. She is standing now, walking, one foot in front of the other. *Good girl.* She takes a high step over the lip of the tub, into the water, sinks right in: it is tepid, punishing. *I'll stand over here.* She spots a set of feet, waiting in their clogs at the door.

(

Out of the bath, she feels cooled, almost renewed, but still shaky on her feet. Her caregiver gives her a stiff towel. *Thank you*, she says, as she turbans another one around her head. *I changed the sheets for you. Take two of these. I'll be back soon.*

Chicken noodle soup from a packet. Jean, her fairy god-mother, stirs it in a Styrofoam cup with a long metal spoon. *It's nothing gourmet or anything.* She says, *Thank you, thank you*; she's forgotten all the other words people use to express gratitude. She points to the limp jeans hanging over the chair. *There's money in there.* Jean doesn't move from her seat. *We can talk about that later.* The granules of stock stick, then dissolve on her tongue. *You're Sky's girl, aren't you?* Jean asks her, biting the nail on her pinky. *I saw you two at O'Connell's the other night. He's a good kid, not too bright, but what can you do? His mom worked here for a while, when he was little. We never really got along, though. We used to give out those little bottles of shampoo, and then I find out she's pocketing them. I told her: Look, hun, I'll give them to you for free. For a while she stopped, but then she was right back at it. She told me: Jean, I just can't help myself, I see those little bottles all lined up and it just comes over me. There are people like that. It's the stealing they need more than the stuff, if you know what I mean.* The voice is like a slow, pleasant stream, and her attention a stick trailing through, dappling its surface.

In the morning, she calls Simon, tells him the fever has broken, she should be back soon. *Good*, he tells her, *good*. A silence stretches between them, then snaps: *Well, come back soon, alright?*

The sound of the television hurts. She mutes it, lets the people move around without their sound. Two grown men are huddling over a baby, trying to figure out how to get a diaper to close. They try, fail, try again; they stick the tabs to the soft skin of the belly. The baby giggles, lets out a spray of urine right between the man's eyes.

She wakes as though from an eternity of sleep. She is famished, hungrier than she has been for weeks. It is bright and brisk outside; two nights inside and she has missed an entire season. Winter has settled here. She teeters over to the vending machine. Nothing appeals to her. She wants a warm meal, something she would make for herself: a beef stew, a lentil soup, a potato roll slathered with good butter. Jean finds her there, staring at the empty coils, the single bag of pretzels desperate to make its descent. *Go back to your room*, she yells at her, maternal, implacable. Later, she comes to her with canned minestrone soup, a stack of sandwiches—white bread with bologna and a smear of yellow mustard—a pack of potato chips. She eats quickly, teenager, bottomless pit. *Your boss called, by the way. Said you called him from this number, and he didn't have your cell*, Jean tells her, clearing the dishes onto a cafeteria tray. *I told him you'd probably be on your feet by tomorrow. I've never liked the look of that man, so superior. I have nothing against foreigners or anything; my mom's side is Italian. Actually, it's his wife I can't stand, the Endicott girl, and she's as American as George Washington. Her family owns a big chunk of this town, old money, but you probably know that already. You'd have to chain me to a tree to get me to spend a minute with that woman.*

On the car ride back to the shop, Jean accepts three twenties but refuses the rest. *My husband says I'm too nice*, she tells her. *I tell him, if it wasn't for that, I'd have left him a long time ago. That shuts him up.* She laughs. *Well, anyway, this is you, Mara. Good luck.* She doesn't want to leave. She coughs, blinks hard, pushes down a current from beneath. She hasn't heard her name in someone else's mouth in weeks. She opens the door and steps out of the car, gives Jean a flaccid, girlish wave.

❝

Mara, a name like a sour apple, an unripe stone fruit. *It's a Jewish tradition*, her mom liked to say, one of her famous lines, a lie, one of many, *a name for the impossible child*. Not a keepsake at all, but a wound inflicted, a suspicion fixed into truth.

The shop is exactly as she left it: quiet, a little bleak. Simon is busy dismantling the espresso machine. He looks up, and in a flash she sees it, his relief, and then just as quickly he returns to his task. *It's you. Good*, he says. A low voice is coming from the speakerphone. *No, I'm not talking to you*, Simon tells it. *I'm talking to my employee. No, I don't want to fill out a form. I've done that already.* He takes both hands and throttles the air. *I want to talk to a real person. I don't care if they are in Delaware or New Delhi, but I know there's someone out there who can help me fix this thing. It's a small problem with the valve. Yes, with the valve. Are you writing this down? I just have one simple question. No, I'm not filling the form out again. If you don't put me through to one of your technicians, I don't know what I'll do. No, that's not a threat. Unless you respond to . . .* He pushes his hand through his hair. One, two, three. Repeat. *Of course not. No. Yes, I do understand that this is your job.*

The fever has cleared and with it, voices have recovered their sound, shapes their distinctness. The thought crosses her mind, blackbird darting across a dismal sky: *I am fond of you.*

(

She is ravenous. When Simon is out on an errand to the hardware store, she eats three pastries back-to-back. All day, he moves around the shop as though this were any other day, not her homecoming at all. He hums a tune; he tinkers distractedly with the machine. She doesn't know what she expected. *I'm so glad you're feeling better. We missed you over here.* She closes her eyes, blots the words out, shoves them out of the tiny frame of her mind.

She moves through her end-of-day tasks: shrouding the olives and sun-dried tomatoes with deli wrap; washing and drying the knives, the cheese slicer, the meat slicer; cutting up the day's leftover baguette and placing it in sealed plastic bags in the freezer. When Simon is back in the storage room, she takes a half-bottle of red and a leftover sandwich and pushes them into her tote.

❨

She has no clothes to wash, but she sits in the laundromat, eating her salami sandwich, drinking red wine from the bottle. If the old man notices, he does not mind. *What's your name?* she asks him. *Ken*, he responds, and looks back down at his book. She is disappointed to find he doesn't ask for hers. He is otherwise occupied: *Romance, On the Rocks.* On the cover, a woman stands on a cliff, breasts trussed up in a corset, long blond mane glistening in the sunset. When Mara is done with the bottle, she dozes off, her head dipping down and then jerking back up.

It is dark, but she senses the change right away, the room a warm embrace. It is newly lived in, not so dreary anymore. She sees the outline of a single mattress stretched out on the floor, a pillow on prominent display. She flicks the lighter on; the flame twitters, then dies. She pulls the cord, leaves the bare bulb on long enough to see: the room is just as it used to be, but with a single mattress, a bag full of blankets, a set of faded floral sheets. This is a coincidence, she thinks, turning the lights back off. There is a sound like a baby burbling in the corner of the room. She moves toward it; the heater is sputtering, hissing, the metal hot to the touch. She tries to think of the opposite of a coincidence, but no word comes up.

Paul would know. He knows the word for everything. The opposite of a coincidence, happenstance, fortuity. He is two years, three months, and seven days younger than she is, but he has shaped his life out of facts, cause and effect, words and their definitions, their antonyms. When they were children, he knew everything that she could not; every detail was a grain of sand falling through the sieve of her mind that he caught. The name of every capital of every country, of every battle ever fought, of every street in their city; every name of every person in their extended family, events in the exact order in which they transpired. He remembered everything. A fortress of facts.

«

A thought wriggling around, worm in her ear: *Simon knows you are here.* For the first time in weeks, she is not afraid. She falls asleep easily, knowing that she is a shape in someone else's field.

She wakes up warm, cozy in the well-worn sheets and heavy blanket. The word is there, waiting, an unpleasant film over her mouth: *a trap*. Not the opposite of *coincidence* exactly, and yet she senses she's got it right. She washes quickly, pulls the sheets and blankets up, tucks her backpack back in its box, makes her way down onto the deserted main street. In the diner, she hides in a corner, back to the door. She eats an entire stack of pancakes drenched in syrup, an order of bacon, some tater tots. It is almost obscene, the thoughtless pleasure she derives from this meal.

«

In the bathroom mirror, she is met by a different woman from the last time she was here. A memory of herself: the face fresh, a little bit soft. Something has been loosened from within: her hair is longer, her bangs falling over her eyes. She looks as she did in her teens, newly aware of her own potential to be seen. For a moment she lets herself think it: This is what Simon must see. She is not displeased.

In the health club, she pays the extra four dollars for two towels. She rinses off, settles into the sauna. She is all alone in the cedar box. She pours a ladle of water onto the coals and watches it sizzle; her feet and fingers tingle, her jaw softens, her mouth opens wide. She lies there, feet propped up on the wall, blood rushing down her legs, past her trunk right to her head. She closes her eyes. She is lightheaded, a pig roasting on a spit, an apple wedged into its snout. They had one at their wedding, she and Lucien, a pig roasting on a spit. Paul and Lucien dug the pit in their jean shorts and caps. *My brother, my spouse*; the words flashed before her, side by side for the very first time, a sudden paradox she couldn't pull apart. *They look like gravediggers*, her mother had said, ever alive to her own dread. It had rained, the pork undercooked in the end, but Lucien insisted it was the best he'd ever had. *More tender this way!* She pours another ladle on the coals; maybe if she stays long enough, she can sweat away every last drop.

In the shop that day, she tries but fails to say thank you, to offer to pay him. *Simon?* she ventures again, when she is sweeping near him. *Mara?* he responds, his tone just an echo of her own: unyielding, vaguely mocking. *Nothing*, she tells him, *forget about it*. This is Simon's own way, she understands, of slipping out of sight.

«

She takes note of his wife's traces in the shop: some rose-scented lotion in the restroom, a stack of hairbands and hairpins under the cash register, a series of lists, notes to self, in handwriting that isn't his. *Quilt for Ella? Acupuncture. Risotto Thursday? Simon: albariño tastes like piss?*

Nights go by. A week and then another. He does not come to see her. Relief with a dollop of disappointment, a peppering of disbelief. What did she think would happen?

《

She used to think she could get any man to fall in love with her. Hah. It was a private game she used to play. *You're it*, she'd say. And then she'd use her singular talent, her dangerous skill: pull just the right thread and watch the whole self unspool.

Her brother told her once, not so long ago, sitting on the edge of her bed, gesturing around himself: *This, here, is reality. Everyone lives here but you.* She couldn't help but laugh at the image he conjured: the whole world packed into the small bedroom.

❨

Slowly, facts accumulate, threads she cannot help but pull together in her mind. She sees it and cannot unsee it: Simon is the saddest man in the world. The sheen over his eyes, the twitch, followed immediately by a sigh. A hard blink: one, two, three times. His right hand, always busy, twirling his wedding band. Sometimes, she sees him mouthing it: one, two, three. Each task in need of a countdown, a revving up. He has a scar, a ding above the lip, which she tracks as he speaks. It punctuates his sentences—comma, apostrophe, question mark.

He makes regular phone calls, huddled on the stool in the backroom. From time to time, a snippet of conversation reaches her. *Yes, my love. My girl. My sweet.* His voice is cheerful, enfeebled by his love; he is speaking to a child. Then, his voice drops, grows agitated—a bow pulled back, taut with want: *I can't. No, of course not. You know that's not what I want.* This time, an adult, his wife. When he returns, he is smiling, a fake, encouraging smile, a mask from which a tired voice calls out: *Onwards!*

(

From time to time, Julian stops by, sniffing around the shop. When he does, she usually tries to hide, to keep him off her scent. But he always searches for her, finds her, continues his investigation. *So, up north? Where exactly? Montreal? Oh lovely! I went there once in the nineties. I remember that underground city, how clever! More strippers per capita than any other town. J'adore!* She recognizes his strategy, which she once used herself: To make your will everyone else's, to expand your body so it contains all other bodies, to find a no and make it into a yes, to find a yes and make it into a no. When he is around, she nods, smiles, throws him a little treat. *If you ever go up there again, I'll give you the list of my favorite places to eat,* she tells him, just so that he leaves her alone.

It is October now. The town has shaken off the last of its summer stragglers, dead leaves falling on a blustery day. A few weekenders, here for leaf-peeping, wincing in the wind. A smattering of tourists, Europeans, Californians. They are often lost, asking for directions to the old granite quarries, to the town's historic properties. They buy the bad wine made nearby, every time. *You can really taste the terroir in this one*, Simon tells them, poker-faced.

«

The fishermen, contractors, farmers, locals come in from time to time, buy wine for christenings, anniversaries. They get what they need, leave right away. Then there are the regulars, reformed city dwellers who live here year-round now, their lives so reconfigured, they bear little resemblance to the originals. Julian used to write operas for the Berliner Oper. Simon was a buyer of antiquities in New York City. Another customer was an anchor on national TV. Mara wouldn't know how to describe the old life from which her new one has been shaped. Hers was a renovation so total, there is nothing left over to compare it to.

She needs a coat, but there is only one clothing store in town. It is run by a woman with very short white hair who wears a black kaftan and large tortoiseshell glasses. She tells her that in her opinion, 789 dollars is a bargain for such timeless elegance.

《

Some mornings now, when she is too cold to walk on the beach, she camps out in the town's clapboard library. She does not read. She cannot get the words to cling long enough to their meanings. She thumbs through a book of photographs taken from very high up. Just the kind her brother would make fun of: sentimental, opium for the idiots. Pink lakes and bright shantytowns, a strip mall almost majestic under a full moon. She can look at them for many hours without growing bored. She likes how everything is made both legible and strange by distance, by such a remove.

Some days, she misses the summer, when she could float around town without a tether, when the days were inconsequential, unstuck from one another, letters floating around mindlessly in their alphabet soup.

«

When she remembers: an image, a sentence, a mood from before, she reminds herself swiftly: That's neither here nor there.

She has only the one pair of shoes, white espadrilles, which have a single hole where the left big toe hits the canvas. When she first arrived, the hole was a pinprick, then in September, a dime, in October, a nickel, and now, in November, a quarter. She can get the whole big toe to poke through.

«

How about a seasonal display? Thanksgiving is in less than a month, Simon tells her. *People go nuts over the dreadful holiday.* And so she spends the afternoon with construction paper, a pair of scissors, and some tissue paper that she wads up into little balls. Outside, she collects the prettiest fall leaves—maple, birch, oak—and places them on the floor of the vitrine. *What is it supposed to be?* Simon asks when she is finished. This is his idea of a joke, deadpan, not a hint of levity in his tone. *A turkey waddling through an autumnal scene,* she explains. He laughs. *It looks like something my three-year-old would make.*

When he laughs, it is like a fissure through solid ice, the sound before the mass splits into two parts. She wants to put her hand over his mouth: *Don't*.

《

In the other life, she would have brought Simon to the storage room, sat him down. *Now, now*, she would have told him, stroking his head, *tell me what's on your mind*. In the other life, she would have offered herself up to him: consolation prize, amuse-bouche, interstitial gift.

She gets a phone call. *It's for you*, Simon tells her, as if she is leading a normal life, as if she is a person who is standing on the other end of a line. *Paul*, she whispers when she picks up the phone, but the voice on the line is deeper than his: *It's me, Sky.* The opposite of Paul. She doesn't hear the rest. Something about a steakhouse and a special on Wednesday nights. *No, I can't. I won't. I have to go.*

《

Who was that? Simon asks, when she is back on the shop floor. *Just some guy*, she says. *Huh*, he responds, looking at her for a beat too long. *You moved something*, he snips, later, but when she asks which thing, he says, *Forget about it, I found it, my mistake.* It is as though he knows that she needs it, this reminder: he sees her after all.

I need a few hours up there, Simon tells her the next morning, pointing to the attic door. A dull knife through the quiet continuity of their shared life. This is the first time he implies it, that she sleeps upstairs, that he knows it. She swallows hard. *Of course, have at it.* He looks newly animate. He has gotten a haircut. Maybe his wife has finally come home.

〔

That night, in the attic room, she notices his improvements right away. He has covered up the insulation with drywall and set up a few mouse traps behind the heater, by the door. She tries to thank him the next day, but he stops her right away. *It's nothing*, he declares.

It's nothing, she has to remind herself every time her mind starts playing one of its long-forgotten tunes.

(

She remembers, in bed, a performance art piece she once watched at a museum in New York City. A young woman is sitting on the subway. The scene is mundane, the woman demure. It's the seventies; the woman's hair is ironed straight, parted down the middle. Suddenly, she opens her mouth very wide, an unpleasant yawn; her hands become involved. She pulls at something from within: cotton wool, batting, the stuffing of an armchair. It is uncanny, this endless recovery, this intestinal unfurling; there is so much more matter in there than seems possible, so much more space in the tiny cavity. Everyone around her is aghast, disgusted.

She finds a photograph tucked between the pages of a book entitled *Wines from around the World!* Simon and his wife dressed up for Halloween, wearing matching mice ears and dark sunglasses. She brings the photo in closer, sees it then: a tiny gray mouse, an infant, their child, curled up in the crook of Simon's arm.

(

Three blind mice. It takes her longer than it should to figure it out.

She feels it all the time now, hand hovering over the open flame, the tantalizing heat. She'd like to ask Simon: *Why did they leave you? Where did they go?*

«

One night, she is put in charge of closing the shop. Julian comes in just as she is pulling down the blinds. *I love your display. It's very Klimt, Kokoschka, Schiele, if they were Yanks. Very tongue-in-cheek.* His eyes are bloodshot. She guesses he's taken a bump or two of cocaine. In the old life, they would have been fast friends, she knows, bound by surface intimacies, by a shared sense of play, of drunken ease. *You're not celebrating, are you? Miserable holiday. It's all this I'm-so-grateful-for-my-family bullshit, that worthless institution. Come on, let's have a drink!*

She concedes. She is tired and she knows Julian won't leave without something to gnaw at. She opens a Gamay. *Subtle, earthy, real,* she wrote on the tag—Simon's words, not hers. She takes a sip. It is too warm, nearly bloody, interior, like tasting yourself on your lover's lips. *Tell me something, Mara! Anything, really, I'm bored out of my wits. Something about yourself.* Like what? *Anything! We're all dying to know why you're here. Or at least I am. Simon's preternaturally discreet, so he'd never let on.* She can't think of where to start. What words are worthy of speech? How to break the dam, shatter the windshield. *I was married once. I still am. I wasn't very good at it.* No one is good at that. *But I was exceptionally bad.* Is that why you're here? She shakes her head, no. That was just the scrim, the husk, the shallow stuff. *My mom is originally from around here. From Bristol, about forty miles north. There's that.* So it's a back-to-the-womb sort of thing? Julian asks. Mara laughs. *I'll have to think about that.*

She could have said: Marriage is like a record skipping, a ship with its anchor stuck beneath a rock. A noose, a straitjacket, a bandage bound so tight, the skin underneath it turns a sickly, wrinkled white. She could have said: Marriage is just a metaphor, for everything we want but cannot preserve within a single life. She says instead: In Russia, she once heard, they swaddle babies so tight, their breath gets caught right at the top of their lungs every time they dare try to cry.

«

She could have said: When you lose a child, you go along with her.

She takes more cigarette breaks. She drinks coffee at every occasion. *You're shaking,* Simon tells her, when she is trying to slice the Parma ham into perfect ribbons. *Let me do it. Sit.* He gestures to the backroom. When he is done, he comes to her with a cup of tea. After she has taken her last sip, she sits there, waiting. For what?

❲

It is Sunday. She can't sit still in her room all the time. There is more and more of her in it: a sweater strewn over a chair, a towel in a pile on the floor, empty wine bottles lined up by the door. She goes outside, tries to think of what to do. But all the roads lead her back to Main Street, to the single drag and its one open business.

Jean is sitting in her corner booth; she greets Mara like a long-lost friend. Jean buys Mara one shot and then another. *Where's your man?* she asks, and it is Simon Mara pictures in her head. *You know, Sky*, Jean clarifies. *He's been going around telling people he's in love with a Parisian. Because you're from Quebec, I guess. I don't think he's ever crossed the state line. He's a pretty dumb kid, but you know that already. Heart of gold. Or maybe silver, I don't know*, she snorts, then laughs at her own joke.

SARA FREEMAN

For a moment, Mara tries it on for size: she the sweetheart of a small-town heartthrob. It is a lie uttered in such good faith. *Jean, you know just as well as I do that Sky's just a kid, and I'm not here for long anyway.* Jean gives her a look. *Everybody says that, but you'd be surprised how you get used to this town.* Her face is so lined and expressive, the skin so thin, nearly opalescent. Mara wants to lean over, to touch the single blue vein pulsing alongside her left eye right down to the jaw. *I've been meaning to tell you how grateful I am. For those days at the motel . . .* Now you stop that, Mara. I did the same as anyone with a heart would do, that's it, that's all, don't get all soft on me. Not you too. Last night my husband was crying like a baby because we were in the car and this stupid Christmas carol came on. He hasn't been the same man since Teddy, but that's a whole other story. I don't think I've told you about him. My son. What did they call it? An impairment. You know, after a trauma to the brain. Wasn't the same. They say that about people and I never really understood it, because I've never been able to be different from what I am. That's me for you. And I just can't believe that's to do with a brain. He died some other way that I don't want to say, but he was someone else totally by then, so he died twice, in a way. Don't look at me like that, girl; your pity isn't going to get me anywhere. Anyway, it's your turn to buy.

One whiskey, two beers, a tequila shot. Like a kind of sick hopscotch.

❨

In the mirror at the back of the bar, she sees it: her reflection, an unwelcome judge, a warped self-portrait. The woman in there has a large, accusing nose and there are two dark wells where her eyes ought to be. *Do I look strange to you?* she asks Jean, pointing to the mirror, but she is dead too, her head resting on Mara's shoulder, a dark spot where the drool has seeped through.

For years, she had the premonition: that Paul would die before her. Baby brother, perfect shadow. He was too good for survival, too precious for time. When they crossed the street, she moved around him so she'd be the first one hit, when he fell asleep, she monitored his breathing, when they rode in their mother's car, she forced him into the back seat. But later, when he was an adult and still alive, still stalked by good fortune, she realized it was an idea she'd borrowed, a hand-me-down from the Salvation Army of false mythologies, from that storehouse of all foreboding, her mother's bleak and singular mind. She remembers her mother grabbing his little-boy frame, pressing it against her own frailty: *I know you're going to break my heart. I just don't know how.*

《

In the morning, she heads straight for the beach, eager to slough off sleep, dreams she can't quite remember. The weather is ominously perfect, the bitter chill of winter nowhere to be found. Modest clouds shift across the horizon—incidental, self-contented. From time to time, she hears the crush of sand behind her, a presence nearby. But when she turns around: nothing. Just empty sand alongside empty road where someone ought to be.

The book of aerial photographs has been checked out. *One minute, while I finish this*, the librarian tells her, eyes stuck on her screen. Mara has never liked a counter, its suggestion of approval and denial, the fixity of a no or of a yes. She follows the uneven shore of the librarian's scalp, white at the roots, further down, a color like ruddy sand. *Yes, unfortunately that one's out. If you'd like to recall it, we can.* But Mara doesn't have a library card to start the process. *You'll need a piece of mail, a fixed address. Proof of your existence, in this town, in this region.* She asks for an exemption; it's an exceptional situation. She's here on an extended vacation. *If we did that for every itinerant person who asked, we'd lose our fine collection.* The librarian is touching her cross nervously with her hand now, bringing it up to her lips. *I'm here for the foreseeable future,* Mara begs. *What if I got my boss to come in? Would that be enough?* But the librarian is adamant, every sentence with its same moralizing lilt: *It would not. I can't make any exceptions. Not for you, or for anyone else either. Those are the rules and I don't make them.*

«

She hates these sorts of petty remonstrances. They remind her of childhood, when the world seemed to dangle from a string and adults moved around with their scissors, cutting on a whim.

She goes to sit down, but from her seat, she can still see her, the librarian standing at attention, fiddling with her tiny cross. She is just like this town: a flag dug into the sand on a windless afternoon. I am not going anywhere, the librarian declares with every slow, prideful movement of her chin.

(

You're so thin-skinned, Lucien used to say. He was right: you sew a self so close to the skin, you can't undo a single stitch without undoing the whole thing.

In the shop that afternoon, she tries but fails to go unnoticed. Every time a customer comes in, she moves to the storage room, holds her breath, digs her nails into her wrists. Let Simon take care of it. *Mara, where are you?* he calls out impatiently after a few customers have come and gone. *I'm here*, she yells. *You can't just disappear on me*, he tells her later, like a parent to a child who has gotten lost, on purpose, in a crowd.

(

At school, you used to have to fling your hand up and declare it: *Present!* Even then, she thought it was a funny custom, a particular form of existential punishment, to have to say it in front of your peers, those malevolent witnesses. One time, she put her hand up and it slipped right out of her: *Absent!* That got her sent straight to the principal's office. *I guess it was wishful thinking*, she told them, trying to explain what had come over her. They did not like that at all.

They often said it at school: *Mara's very clever*. But it wasn't meant to buoy her. Paul was exceptional, brilliant. Even back then, she understood it: you could only ever be what you already were.

〈

One bottle no longer gets her drunk. She takes a white with her upstairs alongside the red; it tastes like flowers warmed-over in the sun. But she still doesn't feel the way she wants, just her stomach churning, her throat stinging. Sleep is a hard surface onto which she has been flung.

In the dream, she walks up to the counter and hands the librarian a gift. It's a pretty box: inside it, the glint of a gold cross. The librarian is overcome. She smiles, tears up. She turns around, lets Mara place it on her delicate neck. She holds it up; she presses it to her lips: *I love it so much*.

«

She used to do this as a child: any time her mother said something vicious, inappropriate, she would press pause, rewind, dub it over in her mind.

In the store the next day, Simon is nearly happy. Tomorrow is Thanksgiving. He is lord of his manor, showing off his domain. There is something unseemly about seeing his rare smile on such naked display. Mara wants to go back to the day before, when it was just the two of them, Simon sulking in his usual manner. There are many new faces, city folks back to their summer homes just for the holiday. He opens a bottle to taste, and then another. He is easy, a sail aloft on a perfect windswept day. A woman comes in, looks around possessively, every item of clothing luxuriously worn in. She stands very near Simon, touching his forearm. *How are you holding up?* He is suddenly softened, dismembered, all his good cheer drained away. He is gripping her arm now. *You're her sister; you tell me what to do.* The sister lifts her head up, looks over at Mara behind the counter, strains a smile. *Who's that?* Mara catches the woman mouthing to Simon in the mirror. *No one, just a girl I hired to help around the shop.*

Later, she finds him, weeping in the storage room. She follows his sound, heavy breathing, his man's mind trying to slow down what is quickening, tightening around him. He has just put down the phone and he is slumped, sitting on an upside-down crate. She meets his gaze: eyes buggy, forehead scrunched. He looks ugly, an ostrich freshly hatched. She fumbles around, trying to remember what she has come here to find. She hovers above him, parental emanation in the caverned stacks of canned goods: aluminum packaging glinting in the bulb's bright light. *I'm good*, he says, his voice trembling. A single tear, followed by another, from the other eye, rare tears, a perfect pair of them. He takes one of his paws and wipes at his left eye. His cheeks gleam prettily. *Onwards!* he says and slowly lifts himself off the crate, shaky on his feet; she takes his hand intuitively in hers. It is softer, more delicate than she expected.

On her day off, she stays inside, until she cannot stand the sound of her own breathing, every one of her movements echoed in the creaking of the floorboards. It is midafternoon when she finally makes her way outside. The streets are empty, the bitter wind defeating the sun's dying efforts. She moves quickly, lifting her hood to cover her ears. She wants to see the houses, the families stuck in their celebratory zeal. Every few windows, she finds it, just what she must be looking for: some innocent tableau. Families at rest. A teenage boy moving around the dining room table, his T-shirt flipped up like a kangaroo pouch, holding a pile of silverware. A group of adults standing near a kitchen island, gossiping, pouring wine into giant glasses. A child playing Lego alone on a living room floor. A thought, like a pebble dropped from a great height: she will not watch Paul's son grow up. She continues to walk until she is there, in front of his house: 21 Summit Road. She moves slowly past the handsome pile, its bright red door. She can see into the living room and beyond it, into the kitchen; the back of Simon's head emerges, his shoulders hunched, his arm bent to the right, bringing a lonely spoon up to his mouth.

The next morning, she wakes with the back of his head on her mind, the tantalizing nape, the particular slope of his shoulders.

❝

All roads lead to Rome. She hates the imperialist construct of this adage, but she knows: if there is a mistake to be made, she will make it.

She could say: *Tell me something about yourself.* This is what other people might do.

«

Instead, when it gets dark, she slinks down into the closed store, looks around. Rummages in the back room for something to cling to: traces, relics from the other life. She finds a book of poems, an attractive red-and-white French edition of *Les Fleurs du Mal*. Inside it, the inscription reads: *I will always love you. Yours, Charlotte. Spring 1998, Cambridge, MA.* The hope, the humiliation of that *always*. All those mistakes made in dumb faith. She closes the book, sets it back, covers it up with a heavy crate of tomato puree.

She dreams of an arm outstretched—hers. Her hand is cupped, waiting for change. There is a presence by her side, winding a bandage around and around the hand, up to the arm. It is getting tighter and tighter at every turn, until the arm is entirely mummified. Then a quick tug at the fingers, a glove pulled off, and just like that: the skin is lifted, an entire sleeve of it lying on the floor by her feet. She picks it up, she balls it up like Plasticine.

《

The next morning, pressure at the temples, squeezing at the throat. That old need, to make the world match her want. Back on Main Street, she stands before one of the tourist shops. Inside, all the world's most useless nautical tchotchkes: pastel buoys, a pineapple clock, anchors stitched onto socks. She finds a rock by her feet, picks it up, considers it: throwing it straight through to the other side. She wants to hear the alarm go off, to see how long it would take for someone to show up. At last, a single decisive act. But then she sees, from the corner of her eye, an elderly couple walking toward her with their identical stride.

Lucien used to say: *We'll be old like that someday*. He used to say there was nothing she could do to make him unlove her. We'll see about that, she always thought.

《

Inside the clothing store, she fingers the cashmere coat, tries it on again. *Sometimes you fall in love and you just have to give in to the call*, the owner says. *This is how much I've got*, Mara declares, taking the fives and tens and twenties from her jean pockets, all wadded up. She doesn't feel ashamed. The owner surprises her, accepting her offer. She counts the twenty-dollar bills with the skill and speed of a croupier. *Three hundred forty-five dollars*, she says, a dour look on her face. *Fine. I'm giving you the deal of the century. I hope you know that*, she says. She doesn't give her a bag or even a receipt. On the bench just out of view, Mara cuts the tags off with her teeth and puts the coat on. It is heavy and warm. She counts the money left over in her back pocket. Thirty-six dollars and change.

Maybe you never loved him at all. Who said that? Lucien's mother, or maybe it was her own. She can't remember now. All she knows is this: they met and within a year they were married. *Lucien and Mara.* Always in that order. The day of the wedding, it was drizzling and his mother kept repeating: *Mariage pluvieux, mariage heureux—Rainy wedding, happy marriage—*between bouts of weeping. In most of the photographs, his mother looks like the bride, her pale dress accentuating every curve, her arm looped decisively through Lucien's, her practiced pose dating back to her short tenure, decades earlier, as an eighteen-year-old Mademoiselle Guadeloupe. *I adored his ex*, she had told Mara, when they were getting ready for the ceremony.

«

No one ever warns you: a wedding is like a dream in which every person you've ever known shows up and whispers: *Don't fuck this one up!*

111

She catches sight of herself in a shop window: she looks a little bit ridiculous. The coat is long and jet-black with a high collar lined with a delicate fur trim. A coat for the city, for a trip to the theater or an expensive dinner.

❨

As a child, she enjoyed stories of transformation, redemption, Pygmalion reinvention. In those stories, once the new self is forged, the other self is vanquished, not hovering near all the time, threatening to reappear, in every gesture, and in every dream, in every slip of the tongue.

The book of aerial photographs is back. She sits in the furthest corner of the reading room, her back to the librarian. She opens the book at random, and within moments, she is lost in a sea of flamingos preening in a lagoon.

«

On another page, a giant scalloped shell sits among red hills, shaped from the runoff of a copper mine, a miracle of waste. Mara moves her finger across the ridges, counts them once and then again, just to be certain of the coincidence. Thirty-seven, one for each year of her life.

She looks up: the librarian has left her post. Without a thought, Mara slips the thick book into the new coat and buttons it back up, walks past the empty circulation desk, down the long staircase and out into the blustery cold. Outside, she can still feel it, that heat at the quick, that familiar prick, an idea finding its shape before she can approve of it. A feeling so old it has no origin. She walks quickly, pressing the hard edges of the book against her waist. When she is just a few hundred feet away from the shop, she starts to run, past the post office and the laundromat and the diner and the bar. As she moves, she feels a smile rising, a giggle loosening, until she is laughing so loudly, a man walking his dog stops and turns around to watch.

«

The average duration of an emotion, her sister-in-law used to like to say, is exactly one and a half minutes.

You did something, Simon tells her when she comes into the shop. He gestures to her hair, her clothes. *You look nice.* She shrugs. *Thanks. I washed my hair, it's probably just that,* she laughs. He is wearing a corduroy blazer today, and he has shaved, the first time in many weeks. She can see one or two nicks at his jaw, a forgotten dark patch near the ear.

༄

That night, after the shop is closed, she tells him: *I don't want to go up there yet. I don't think I can bear it.* Simon flips open a chair at the long fold-out table. *Sit, please.* He stands before her, wipes three glasses, and lifts them up to the light. Satisfied, he opens three bottles: one white and two reds. He pours. She swirls, sniffs, tastes, swallows. She closes her eyes. *Green apple, silt, somehow beneath it all, some salt.* And then another sip. *Volcanic. Rose hip, or maybe anise?* A final swallow. *Cranberry, a little too bright at the top.* Three big sips and she feels tipsy, with him watching her like this, her tongue returned to her like a gift.

They get drunk. Just the two of them. They finish the first two bottles, then turn to the third. *Charlotte would kill me. She made me quit when our daughter was born*, Simon says, pointing dismissively at the heaped ashtray between them. *But she's not here to murder me anymore.*

«

This is a border crossing, foreign territory, something akin to intimacy.

The next morning, the winter light is like a cold blade through the pale butter yellow of the room. The wine they drank was very good, so she wakes up fresh, untarnished by the night.

(

Julian comes in when Simon is in the storage room. *How is he?* he asks. He speaks in a low whisper. *I heard you got him drunk. Good on you! I worry about him, our Simon, a hard-shelled, soft-bellied creature. She said she'd be back by Christmas and of course, now she's saying Easter. Well, thank god you're around, Mara. Take his mind off things for a while.*

It is December now. Nobody has come to save her. The fact solidifies beneath her, a layer of black ice under every thought.

〈

In the library, she moves on to a book on pointillism. Seurat, Signac, Cross. *Oil paints are de rigueur in this novel technique. The thick texture allows for less bleeding, blurring, running.* She enjoys one of the Seurats most: the quiet repose of boys lounging on the bank of their dotted river. She turns the page. A self-portrait of Chuck Close, which she draws near to her nose and then pushes away.

He died once. Paul. But only for a few minutes. They had been sent to camp that year, the summer of their father's desertion. There was a drill one morning, an announcement made over the intercom: A camper is missing! A camper is missing! Hundreds of children buzzing around the flagpole. Nervous laughter. A child missing, a child dead. These seemed like funny matters back then. Children didn't die. Even Mara laughed into her cupped hand, picturing something so absurd, adults letting this kind of thing happen to a child. She looked around for Paul. Even here, he was always nearby, always within arm's reach, her shadow. And then a fact before it becomes one: he was the missing child, the dead child. His name, *Paul*, on all the children's lips. She wanted them to stop saying it; it was her name to say. If one more person says it, she thought: That's it, he's dead. And then there was talk of the docks, swimming. The camp counselors, tanned saints, sex incarnate, diving in, one after the other, bathing suits splintering red against the dark lake. The sound of a whistle and then another and another, a deafening orchestra of channeled breath. They carried him out on a stretcher. It was him, only dead. She went straight to the body and had at it, hitting it on the shoulder and across the face. And then a smile appeared, his. Cheering from the other children. His teeth, laughing, oversized in his mouth, crowded at the front. *It was just a drill, Mara*, a voice trying to calm her down from above. But she wasn't done. She took her hands to his neck, pressed her weight into the tender flesh, until the counselors had to pry the siblings apart.

For weeks afterward, she refused to look at him. She understood just what her mother had meant with her broken refrain: what he could do to them, what he could take.

(

Simon gives her the list of holiday tasks, which she tackles without a word. Quince jelly, Manchego, Marcona almonds, a box of oatcakes. She wraps the whole thing up in a crinkly plastic sleeve, ties a paisley bow around it. Repeat. *You look bored*, he tells her when she is done with the holiday baskets. *I don't get bored*, she lies.

Everyone who comes in says it: *Only two days left!* They all need it, this countdown, this raison d'être. Simon moves around fretting about this and that, a bottle of Carignan he can't locate, a special order of a dozen panettone that hasn't arrived. They will be closed for only a few days and she is glad for it. She wouldn't know what to do with such a large expanse of time, without the quiet rhythm of the store: wrapping and sweeping and shelving and slicing, the sound of Simon moving nearby. She suspects that the same is true for him.

☾

Julian stops by on his way to a holiday party. He is dapper with his red bowtie, his green suspenders. He winks at her, kisses her on both cheeks, calls her *darling*. She is fond of him now. Simon opens a bottle of Cava. Not a fresh burst, but like hay and sun and chamomile. *This one reminds me of me*, Julian says, pleased with his own joke. Simon opens another bottle, white this time. *This one is like that boyfriend I had who had ADHD.* Julian insists on knowing everyone's plans. *I'm still on the fence about whether or not to go home*, Mara says. She sees something flash in Simon's eyes; he has caught her in her lie. He knows her better than he lets on.

Simon opens another. A red this time: cherries before they become too sweet. *What do you think?* It's just the two of them now. She likes it, she tells Simon, but it begs to be forgotten, doesn't linger long enough to make its mark. He is pleased with this description. *I agree. Bit of a tease.* She is close enough to see it, scar on the lip, a perfect ding twitching as he says her name. A skip, a heartbeat. A hand waving her over. *I meant to tell you: we're running out of Bleu D'Auvergne*, she declares, getting up too quickly. She takes the thin slab of blue cheese out from the case and unwraps it. She feels its acrid, metallic smell deep inside her nose. She lifts it up. *See, it's nearly done.* He gets up, comes around the counter and looks down at it, his eyes smiling. *I see*, he says. *I'm very glad you told me this important news.* He is standing so near her, she can smell the cigarettes and wine and something else, warm and unknown. They look down at the cheese case for a very long time. She is the one who grabs for his hand. How long does it take for him to move it away, to press it to her shoulder, to say something about getting home, early bird gets the worm, and it is gone, and she is all alone again, metal banister on her bare hand, skin raw against the woolen blanket?

That night, those lips return. Their pale, dried-out, mannish pink: the smallest movement of the apostrophe, a hand waving her over. She finds that rush of heat from within, sensation returned, old friend. She stops just before she climaxes; she hears skittering beneath her, between the floorboards, manic rustling, a mouse. She is not scared, just aware of the little body scurrying near hers. Mice, she once heard, use the traces of their urine like maps, to find their way back to the nest, trails of themselves leading right back to themselves.

«

In the shop, he looks at her without the whisper of a change. He is good at this, she thinks, stashing dangerous knowledge on the highest shelf. Or perhaps she is the one who has gotten it all wrong.

She opens up a tin of sardines, the slick little bodies lying perfectly snug in their aluminum cot. *This, here, is reality.*

⟨

All day, customers come in and out. He walks past her, moves his hand through his hair, twirls his wedding ring, picks up a receipt and places it next to her without a word or glance. How little she figures in his mind's eye! What will it take? She pictures the top of her finger sliced off, his hand stopping up the blood, or better yet, her body floating in the bay, her belly taut, Simon wading in, gathering her up.

In the early afternoon, she sees them out the window: the addicts from months before. They are discussing something important, talking very loudly, their voices carrying indoors. The man looks worse than before: the skin on his face forms a milky casing around the cheekbones, the forehead, and jaw. But the woman looks the same. For her, time stands still, a song stuck on repeat: the agitated look of her eyes, the searching disquiet of her hands. She moves away from him, leans against the shop window, crouches down, takes a discarded cigarette butt and lights it, takes one drag and stomps it out again. From the side, Mara sees it: the rounded belly pressing out. A mother is always a daughter before she is a mother, the thought emerges, already formed. The girl does not have a coat, just a sweater, with sleeves that fall short of her wrists. Mara can feel Simon hovering behind her, ignoring her. Everything he does seems to suggest it: she is nothing to anyone anymore.

《

She grabs her coat from the hook at the front of the store, runs out the door. She is outside now, handing the coat to the pregnant girl. *It's yours*, she says, *have it, I don't need it anymore*, she says, turning back before more words can be formed. When she comes back into the shop, Simon looks up but doesn't say a word.

They close early. Simon opens a bottle, pours her a large glass. *What did you do that for?* he asks. *Give away your new coat like that?* She drinks, waves his attention away. *I don't know. She looked cold, and she's pregnant, you know, poor girl . . .* She thinks of the hoodie from the road, the one she has on. She wants to change the subject; she asks about his Christmas plans. But he doesn't want to let go. *I have all these clothes my wife never got around to giving away and you had just bought that coat, hadn't you?* he asks again. He is growing agitated now: he is moving closer to her, a new insistence in his eye. *I just don't understand you*, he says. She senses a brightening around her; it is the first time in many months that she is under any real scrutiny, an object lifted to the light. *What does it matter to you what I do?* she asks. His face is flushed now, looking up at her, the entire world cracked open between them. She has wanted this, this fracture, and now that she has it, she does not. She steers the boat back to dry land, asks again about his Christmas plans. *My sister is coming over. We're not very close, but I think she pities me now, what with my situation, an unwilling bachelor. I think it suits her that way. And you? Any siblings? I've never asked.*

Only child. She answers so quickly, it doesn't even feel like a lie. She lets the thought of it settle in: him without her, her without him. But it's a strange experiment, a body without its spine, a sea with no tide.

❝

I wish you'd told me you had nowhere to go, Simon tells her, not looking her way. They say goodnight, and as they do the thought floats up and instead of letting it go, she spits it out: *I just wanted to see what would happen. You know, if I gave the coat away. Do you know that feeling?* He looks embarrassed, standing there at the bottom of the outdoor staircase. *Not really*, he says, and digs his hands in his pockets. She laughs: *I guess it's just me, then.* He looks up at her and she sees it, unbidden, a smile, his reflexive delight, salvaged from long before. She walks up the stairs. *Goodnight*, she says, not looking back, but she knows he is standing down there, still as a rock.

You always fill your drink right up to the top, Lucien used to say. *And then you act surprised when it spills everywhere.*

❨

It is Christmas morning, and she remembers: she is all alone in the world. She wraps the blanket around her shoulders and goes downstairs with a cup of tea, the leftover half of a glazed doughnut, her pack of cigarettes already nearly smoked. Not a soul on the road. This is exactly what she wanted, she must remind herself: to slip into a blind spot, to run out on her life.

For dinner, she warms up a can of baked beans on her hotplate and covers them with a layer of grated cheddar. She eats the whole thing straight out of the pot, chasing it with a bottle of Brouilly. She has nothing to occupy her, no safe thoughts to keep her company. It is snowing outside, and she crouches on the bed, her nose up against the cold windowpane, watching the clots making their descent. She spots one as it catches on a thin branch and splits into two parts.

(

There was a game they used to play as children, she and Paul: I am you and you are me. Paul would answer to *Mara*, and Mara to *Paul*. They played for days, until their mother, worn thin, finally gave in to their game. Mara would be Paul, and Paul would be Mara. They played as if they belonged to no one, to nothing. Even their parents were irrelevant; their father a sudden absence, a fact to move around, their mother an omnipresence, unruly ocean to their raft. It was just a game they invented: I am you and you are me.

Later, babysitters, teachers, relatives would declare it: how little they had in common, how opposite they were. If she was tall and wraithlike, then he was short and strong. If he was a good egg, then she was a bad apple. If he was a bright auditorium, then she was a dimly lit corridor. If he was fully realized, exemplary, then she was pure potential, an energy not yet forged into its singular shape.

«

But it didn't really matter until her sister-in-law came along. She had come to their family as an anthropologist, an envoy from the land of the adjusted, notebook in hand, pencil sharpened to a violent point. *Enmeshed*, that was her conclusion, after months of observation, Paul reported back to Mara. She had a way of using the ugliest possible word to describe each thing, twisting what was pure into something tawdry.

She can feel it, the past, grabbing, pulling. Not the recent years, no; it is the distant past that draws her in. She does not flail around. It takes her wherever it wants her to go; this is the mind's undertow.

《

She was a child who loved repetition. She liked her father to say certain words to her, repeat them over and again. They didn't need a sentence to house them, just those sounds in his mouth, rolling around and around, until they'd been dulled of their flavor, their sense. *Matinée, rococo, urticaire, anarchie, annuaire.* He rolled his *r*'s with his particular regional panache. It made his mustache quiver, his tongue curl. And then when he couldn't stand it anymore, he'd clap his hands. *Ça suffit, ma belle.* But that was after what felt like hours of play. *That's enough, my love.*

She spoke only her father's language then, their language together. She could spell every word and conjugate every verb. She was very intelligent. An intelligent child. He said it and so she knew it. He was her witness. Her mother didn't witness a thing. She wasn't like a mother at all. She was the weather system under which they lived, a sudden gust followed by an eerie period of calm, a sunny day made terrifying by what might follow, by what had come before.

(

That was before he disappeared, before every scrap of French, of his Christianity, were banished from the house. When he left, he took Mara's language, all her meaning with him, every last verb, every single tense she'd ever learned. *I will not have the language of the oppressor here!* her mother used to like to declare in those days, inverting the logic of the local politics.

There are those who leave and there are those who are leftover. That was her mother's favorite phrase in those days.

⟨

You could have tried harder to get your father to stay, her mother used to like to remind her.

Runs away with her thoughts, a note on her report card once read. Now, thirty years on, she supposes she's done exactly that. She's run away, and her thoughts have come with her, trailing behind, always nearby.

❦

Sometimes she pictures it: her life stripped of certain phrases, her mind rid of its particular rhythm, its meter. But it is nearly impossible to unlearn a language. Even when you think you've lost it altogether, it floats up to the surface, refusing to be swallowed down. The syntax stays, the grammar survives, the order your mind makes out of all those orphaned words.

She is floating at the surface of sleep when she hears it, his knock at the door. It is Christmas still, she thinks. Paul has finally come to find her. He has never let her down; how could she forget this? She runs to the door, pushes her hair back, opens it up. She nearly cries when she sees him: Simon standing in the doorway. *Come in*, she says. *I've caught you at a bad time. You were sleeping.* He looks forlorn, a sad Santa, holding a drooping cardboard box in his arms. *I can't bear her anymore, her schadenfreude. Schaden-sister, that's what I should call her. She leaves tomorrow, thank god. I brought you this stuff. I was thinking of throwing it out.* He takes each item out and shows it to her: a short puffy jacket, some gloves, a scarf, some boots, a pair of jeans, two woolen cardigans, a stovetop espresso maker, everything nearly new, his wife's things. She brings the scarf up to her nose: bergamot and something spicy, clove or maybe ginger, faded, persistent.

May I? He sits on the bed; his body stiffens. It is strange, to have him so near, after all these weeks of keeping him right out of arm's reach. *I don't really know what I'm doing here*, he says, mid-sigh. *I'm an idiot. I thought they'd come back today. I was sure of it.* He sits beside her, leans his head on her shoulder; it is heavy with sorrow, everything kept dutifully in. She regrets it already, the decision that is about to be made. But just as quickly, a stronger tide comes along: desire insisting quietly on being met. She runs her hand through his thick hair.

«

She is the one to kiss him. A shut door he slivered open that she kicks in. He pulls away: *I have to go. My sister will be waiting.*

Stay, she says, holding her arms out like a child.

)

For a moment, after he is gone, she wonders if she can bear it: another night spent alone.

She wraps herself in his wife's scarf and coat. *This* is not the end of *that*, she knows. A song recognized, unforgotten. She thinks of Simon, falling asleep to this very same smell: bergamot and something spicy, ginger, maybe, or clove.

«

Outside in the brisk morning, she moves through the streets in his wife's hand-me-downs, the wind hissing in her bare ears. On Main Street, she sees him everywhere. The back of a head in the pub, the look of a pant leg moving around a corner, a man's bare hand holding a child's mittened paw.

The lights are on in the store when she returns. Simon is there, standing with his arms akimbo, studying his wares. She makes her way indoors. *Hello there!* he calls out. He hopes he didn't scare her, he's just here to get a bottle of wine for a dinner at Julian's, he explains, too emphatically. *You can come, if you'd like, if you have nothing else on, of course,* he says. *My sister's gone.* She hears it, behind his untrained tone, his want.

«

The party doesn't start for another hour. *We'll go upstairs and drink up there*, she tells him. *I don't know*, he says. *But I do*, she replies. How right it feels to tell him so: like stealing back into a still-warm bed.

It's kind of like college, Simon says, gesturing to their scene: two grown bodies sitting side by side on a mattress on the floor, drinking red from the bottle. *I wouldn't know*, she says, tonelessly. Simon gives her a look of earnest apology. *You couldn't have known. I spent one semester there; that was enough*, she laughs. *I'm sorry*, he says, *I didn't mean to assume.* He takes a sip, wipes the lip with his sleeve, and passes it back to her. *You're shaking*, she tells him, steadying his long fingers with her own. *You're not scared of me, are you?* He shakes his head. *Not exactly.* He laughs a little, looking down at his feet. *Maybe.* He grabs for the bottle, takes another swig.

(

I'll be very gentle, she says, like a mother to a child.

This is not me, he tells her when they are lying on the bed, kissing, stroking each other. *If it's not you, then who is it?* she laughs. He refuses to take off his clothes, to let her take hers off either, so they are like teenagers, rubbing jean on jean, until it doesn't seem like a body could contain any more heat. *Simon*. His name is in her mouth; she senses it already disappearing, already out of reach, a soft call from the deepest place, dead and now drifting. *I'm going to take this off*, she tells him quietly. She lifts the shirt above her head, unclasps her bra, moves the soft pads of his fingers over the nipples, lets them perk up. He presses his lips to the hard cone of flesh, licks slowly and then hungrily, discovering his own need. Even his loneliness has its limits, even such pride needs its respite.

«

She is like a wound, gauzed over. And now the big reveal. Dampen the bandage with water, peel it off, careful not to take with it too much of the stuck skin. Remove the bandage, look inside: the dried-up blood, the yellowed pus. Here beneath it: a new skin, tight around the seams, tender to the touch.

Things happen as they do only in the dark, a plant inching toward the light, a language forgotten and recalled, an intuition subtly confirmed. She finds it again, undisturbed, her pleasure. It strikes her, as he moves inside her, close and heavy, hovering mystery above her, that this might be the only story she's ever known: desire and its temporary salve.

In the morning, she wakes to his naked back, the tantalizing nape, the particular slope of his shoulder. She takes note: this is the quietest room in the world. When she is alone in it, every noise is full of its own possibility, its terror, but with Simon by her side, every creak and tug of the house glides right off her skin, inconsequential in its neutrality. She is the house, the roof, the eaves, and the beams. He wakes and turns. He opens one eye and then another, smiles at her, closes them again. He moves toward her, his hands searching. She is a girl running barefoot in a field—untethered, entirely at ease. She is the field itself, with its tall grasses swaying, the soft pad of feet flattening the blades, springing back up with uncomplicated ease. Such soft joy. There is nothing he could do that would not please her. Simon is above her; it takes her a moment to remember him, to put the pieces together again. Now and then. She wants to say, *I love you*, to no one in particular. Instead, she tells him, *Fuck me harder.* He moves his hands along her flanks. *I want to*, he says, but he continues as he has, gentle current above her. She sees it in her mind's eye: a stream in the woods with a tree pulled up nearby, its roots caked with clods of dirt, shuddering in the breeze.

They are good lovers. They spend the day in the attic room, discovering this fact together. She'd forgotten that every time a new story begins, it feels like the only beginning, the real one after all the false ones, those dress rehearsals for what was to come. She doesn't want this story to be over. *Read it to me one more time*, the child in the library begged his mother the other day, still pages away from the end. In this room, there is no past to reckon with, no cast of characters to move around on her mind's stage: just the two of them, making a world out of sheets and limbs and pillows and tongues. Neither of them mentions the party they missed the night before, or the store, that it ought to be open, that they are up here hiding instead. This is his specialty, his gift, she thinks, the inquisitive tongue, the curious hands.

«

All of those months wasted as strangers, she tells him, kissing his neck, his ears, placing his thumb in her mouth, sucking it like her own. They speak this way, as if they have always known one another: as if they are alone with themselves, no explanations necessary. *I never imagined*, he says, but when she asks him what, he says, *I don't know. Never mind, come here, you're so far away.* He pulls her in and they begin again stitching and unstitching and restitching again.

Night falls and he goes out and returns with provisions: two souvlakis, a bag of chips, and some wine from downstairs. *I felt like everyone was looking at me differently, as if everyone knew what I had done*, he says, all of his innocence on bashful display. He eats absentmindedly, his wedding ring glinting. He is nervous again, his left eye twitches. *Know that I don't expect a thing*, she says.

«

Lucien used to say: *You won't be happy until you've burned the whole house down.*

With Simon around, Lucien returns to her. One lover and the other. Where Simon is tentative, shy even, Lucien was unabashed in his desire, heavy with it, as though he wanted to press what they had between two large panes. Simon is very serious, diligent, nearly technical about her pleasure, deferent about his own.

《

When she first met him, Lucien, the word *husband* floated above his head like a banner; she had heard that he was someone else's. She worked at the restaurant where he was a manager, wanted from the beginning to be near him, his husky joie de vivre, his equanimity with a twist. Every time they spoke, she felt it, beneath his affability: that wall, that boundary, a line she was being asked not to cross. It was not just his wife that she sensed, always nearby, but something deeper, fortified over time, his own. How could she explain it? That there was something whole that she wanted severed, something clean she needed soiled?

It took some skill. She listened with the practiced patience of a willing stranger: making patterns out of his past, symmetries out of his life. A mother as enamored as a wife, a wife as kindly as a mother; an easy marriage with an older woman, the impossibility of a child between them. Every story he told, Mara understood as pure prelude to whatever the future between them might hold. She persisted for months. And then she finally noticed it, the slow unstitching, speech between them a kind of undoing. His wife's name slowly disappeared from his mouth, a tentative *she* instead. And then a space made between them, Lucien and Mara, for everything they had in common. What they were like as children: scrappy, daydreamers. Their fathers' long shadows: his had died when he was twelve; hers she'd simply murdered in her mind. They'd both found it around the same time, what was closest at hand: drinking, sleeping around. Precious balm, amnesia on demand.

Now every day spent in the shop side by side is a secret she and Simon hold: a clandestine fort, a shoebox stashed under the bed. Sometimes, they find each other in the musty backroom. They kiss and touch, and when the bell rings to announce a customer, he tells her: *You go first, I'll follow, I don't want to be responsible for any heart attacks*, pointing down to the proof of his want. When he finally joins her, she sees him as he really is: flushed, and happy, a little forlorn. Sometimes when they are together, he reminds her: *You know, they could come back any minute and then this will have to stop*, as if there is no difference between a year, a month, a week, or an hour.

Walking along Main Street one evening, he tells her, *This place used to be only hers. Now with you in it, I'm not so sure anymore.*

)(

She sees it now: glint in his eye, her own reflection.

A habit begins to find its form. Each night, Simon opens a bottle and turns over two milk crates. *Sit*, he tells her. *I want you to taste this.*

《

She regains the old appetite, prepares her favorite meals from before: *cacio e pepe,* sardines on toast, a simple endive salad. When she smells her clothes now, they smell of her again, warm and familiar, a little like Simon, and something unknown, the future, maybe. When she looks in the mirror, she sees a fresh glow at her cheeks; it is winter, but there is summer right beneath, a current of it under a thin layer of ice.

I was dead before, she thinks, waking up with him in the yellow glint of the attic room.

☾

In bed one night, when they are tired out and nearly bored, he explains about the tides: the forces of the moon and sun, their endless tug of war. *Some of the earliest tidal mills*, he begins, propping himself up onto his elbows, *date all the way back to the seventh century*. He tries to describe the mechanism to her, the rush and release of water, the churning of grain into flour, but she knows that later, she'll remember this instead: the tendon in his neck straining as he talks, the clavicle lifting like a lock, the Adam's apple bobbing as he swallows. This is what she'll picture from now on when she thinks of the tides.

He does not invite her over to his house. It's a small town, and some of his wife's relatives live nearby. But Mara doesn't mind, not much, at least; she'll take what she can get. She isn't thinking about the future now, some story already told, already in the midst of its undoing. In the evenings, he comes to her without fail, smelling of soap and something waxy, like the inside of an old coat. Sometimes, they make love and fall immediately asleep, holding each other. Sometimes, he traces her collarbone absentmindedly with his finger, talks about the other life, the one without her in it. He is only forty, but he speaks as though he is very old and has traveled a long distance to end up here with her.

When he says her name—his wife's name, that is—he is tentative, uneasy, as if to speak it between them is a form of blasphemy.

(

It is a bleak winter; gray sky meeting gray sea, gray brush edging gray rock. Even the snow seems somehow muted, starving for the light.

She finds that she can read again. Words have been returned to themselves. She cannot stand the thought of a novel, all that history, all those words spoken out loud, love and family and hope, overlapping, intersecting, invariably chafing, bruising, breaking. She finds a few poems instead: a caught fish, mussed sheets, a sleeping infant, rendered in their perfect mystery, then just as quickly disappeared. This is exactly what she wants to read: a few clouds drifting steadily out of scene. It's the echo she wants more than the sound.

(

Julian finds out about them and says with a sad laugh: *Good on you, girl. Enjoy it while it lasts!*

She has the dream again, the same one she's had for all these years. In it, she is in love with Paul. Nothing happens in the dream; it is all aftermath, cleanup, the shame that comes with such a fact. In the dream, they are teenagers. She has long hair and bangs, and he is chubby, fresh-faced, eyes a startling green. In the dream, it has already happened, what inevitably happens between them in these dreams. Neither of them will say what it is: theirs is a world of secrets, knowledge stowed away, unseen. The knowing is the dream, the backdrop and foreground, the air they breathe, the light that holds them. She wakes, and for a minute, she knows nothing, remembers no one, no comforting fact, no alleviating counter-fact. She turns around and Simon is next to her, earthly solidity, his hair in a funny puff of sleep. Afterwards, she can't close her eyes. She is scared of sleep, that world of parallels and suggestions, infinite regress, all those objects, homesick for their lost meanings.

Sometimes Simon says: *I wish things were different; that we had met at a different time, or better yet, that I could live two lives, one with you in it, the other with them by my side.* When he says it, she wants to cry. When he says it, she wants to tell him: *I already know every story's end.*

Why did you lie? About being an only child? he asks, one night when she mentions her brother, Paul. *It seemed easier than to explain*, she ventures. She tries to tell him about them: her mother, her father, her husband, her brother, his wife, the child she lost. But each time she begins, she hears just how it will sound: every detail an excuse, every fact a worn-out proof. She sees it, the way pity gathers like pleasure around Simon's eyes, how he will think of her: sick branch on a sick tree.

《

It used to comfort her, her family's history, the brutal fall of that regime. She used to think, if *this* happened, then of course *that*.

He's the one who needs to get it off his chest, to talk about his wife, his cumulative loss. *College sweethearts*, he recalls. From the day they met, he confesses, they spent every night together, took every class together. Every fact they learned belonged to the other; they lived this way for many years. Maybe that was the trouble. At first, it seemed that together everything could only grow, become fuller. He had never expected such good luck, a gangly boy from a midwestern suburb, the eldest of two, son of a single mother, Lebanese-Armenian immigrant, who spoke only enough English to get by in her job waxing the upper lips and bikini lines of suburban moms. And this girl, Charlotte, white as a supermarket egg, who told him she'd never had a single bad day, not one. And then, fifteen years in, she was the one to lose her grip, to feel it slip out from under her, the entire structure of their lives, the apparatus of her belief. The worst of it was, he had gone along with every single suggestion, every single prescription, every adventure she'd proposed. He watched her make love to strangers, spent weeks on silent retreat. He had even agreed to leave everything behind in New York City to come here, to the place where she had spent her summers, to the town her family practically owned. That had been her idea, five years ago now. *Now she's back in New York, doing god knows what*, Simon said. *Sometimes I think she moved us here so she could have the city to herself. But I can't get myself to resent her. Not really, anyway. She's the love of my life*, he tells her.

What about this? Between us? He is quiet for a very long time, his hand moving ever so slowly through his hair, before he utters it, his conclusion, his expert opinion: *Parallel universes.* She pictures the two realities like this: the straight tracks of cross-country skis cutting through fresh snow.

(

We'll burn that bridge when we get to it. That's what Lucien had said. He was someone else's husband then and she had asked him: *What happens when you fall in love with me? What happens to us then?*

Not *if* but *when*.

‹

She finds another photograph of them, stashed under the counter, inside a cookbook, between recipes for cassoulet and chickpea fritters. Simon is in the picture, but he is much younger, not yet grown into his limbs, his nose. His arm around her waist, loose and yet proprietary. Charlotte wears her long red hair down her back; she is pushing away his left hand. *Don't.* Her eyes are distant, gazing on. She is already angling to get out of the frame.

He loves her. She knows it now. They take long, frigid walks along the beach, and if there is no one else around, she slips her hand in his coat pocket, gathers his dry fingers in hers. *Can you believe something so small could feel so good?* he asks, and looks at her, as though she has taught him the wickedest trick.

(

B and *A* is *BA*. Easy as that.

Simon does not speak about his daughter. When Mara asks about her, he tells her: *No, I can't talk about* that.

‹

She pictures it sometimes, calling Paul. *It's me, Mara*, she'll say. *You won't believe how much I'm changing.* Or better yet: *You wouldn't even know I was me anymore.*

She hears Simon one morning, talking on the phone in the back room. She can't make out what he is saying, but she senses the sound, the gentle familiarity of it, the tone he uses when he is with her in bed. *Everything alright?* she asks, when he reappears. He nods, smiles. *Fine, everything's perfectly fine.*

Sky comes in a few days later, when she and Simon are both in the store. He does not greet her, but stalks around the shelves, touching the packaging, the thin necks of the bottles. *So you do sandwiches here?* he asks Simon, his voice unnaturally loud, pointing to the chalkboard outside that reads *Sandwiches*. He is dangling a pair of keys from his middle finger, fiddling with them loudly. *Mara can help you*, Simon says dispassionately, pointing to the counter. *So how filling are they?* Sky asks, looking down into the case, ignoring her entirely. The prosciutto is drooping out of the sandwich provocatively; she'd like to lean down to push it back in, hide it inside its bread. *Because, you know, I hate false advertising.* He has an insidious little smile now, his hair pomaded down the middle, his pupils threatening all the white space. There is the counter between them, but he is still too near. She would like it to stop. The whole thing. The entire causal order that has led her right here. He is not here for a sandwich at all. This fact suddenly seems like a dangerous thing. She looks around, but Simon is gone, decamped to the storage room. *I think you should leave now, Sky.* He shrugs, and for a moment he leans his head back, and she is certain that he is gathering his spittle, preparing his assault. But he simply swallows, makes a grunting sound, and leaves the store, the bell clanking angrily in his wake.

When Simon comes back, she is shaking. *Never do that again.* He looks at her, bewildered. *Do what?* He is a little boy thrust into the world of adult stakes. *Leave me like that, in the store, with a guy like that.* He stands in place, stock-still; he does not like to make mistakes. *I'm sorry,* he says half-heartedly. But she can tell that this is not what he had in mind: his loyalties, his sense of duty, are still deployed elsewhere.

(

The surface of their interaction is intact, but she senses it, every single fact from before, pulling him back into position.

One night, he does not come to see her. The first night in nearly sixty days. She waits and worries. When it is midnight, she goes outside into the late winter night. The trees are so still and so bare, nearly mocking, enticing her to misbehave. She has a cigarette and then another, considering it: walking over to his house, tapping on the window, demanding everything all at once: an explanation, a declaration of his intent. She has been, up until now, so well-behaved, a paragon of grace. In the shop that afternoon, everything seemed normal again. He even put on a Leonard Cohen song and told her, *This one reminds me of you*, as if they were two college sweethearts with their whole lives left to spend under the auspices of their favorite song. She goes to the bar instead. Sky is not there, Jean either. Only Donaugh, the old drunk, humming and drooling, all alone. She has a whiskey and then another. She knows, as she has always known, before things can be known: *this* is the end of *that*. She drinks until her mind is empty enough so she can go upstairs, lie on the bed fully clothed, face flat against the mattress, to die on her own.

Paul, of course, disapproved of the whole union. Mara and Lucien. Tearing a marriage apart, and for what? For a fresh surge of pheromones, a few months' whim. It seemed like a recipe for grief, he reasoned with her, the very same idiocy that had brought about their own family: a connection forged on sheer fantasy, on unchecked stupidity. But everything was already set in motion by then, forbearance entirely beside the point.

And then there was her sister-in-law. Paul met her within days of hearing about Lucien, as though only his sister's love could plant the seed of his own.

«

I wish you were half as interested in me as you are in them, that's what Lucien used to say about Paul and his wife.

She wakes in the afternoon, flattened out, a paved road on which large trucks drive their heavy cargo. Simon has not come to find her. She closes her eyes, tries to unlearn what she has known: his gentle tongue meeting hers, that heat at his chest, that dent where the ribs meet and then part. These are not facts but mere sensation, a mirage she imagined and now must unimagine, untack from her corkboard.

《

She is right, of course; she knows everything before it can be known, her fate granted in premonitions, in dreams. She does not leave the room. She eats fistfuls of stale popcorn. She sleeps early, her belly rumbling, waiting for him to descend on her, to declare that the time is here: she has overstayed her welcome.

She is not asleep when he arrives, but she keeps her eyes closed anyway. He stands above her, father about to take his leave. *You know I care about you*, he tells her. She has heard this one before, her father's parting call, etched in bone. He is shaking her gently and then more vigorously: *Mara, you have to get up now.* His eyes are dark pools of regret. *I care about you too*, she wants to say, but instead she mutters, *Fuck you, Simon, I'm sleeping. Whatever it is, it can wait.* He shakes his head, blameless child, battered little boy. *This can't wait*, he says. *It just can't. I can't.* His coward's manifesto. *They're back. Lottie, my Ella. You have to leave tonight.* She gets up; her heart is pounding so fast but there is something nearly good about it, sweet even, her life's suspicion neatly met: kicked out, evicted, disappeared.

(

Fifteen minutes and the room is returned to itself: a square of dispossessed land, a squatter's paradise.

The car clock reads 1:13 a.m. She has been here before. In this exact tug-of-war. Wedged between a man and his wife. *Just tell me what to do*, Simon says, *where to take you. I'm so sorry, Mara. I just, I don't know what else to do.*

❨

You'll leave her, that's what you'll do. That's what she said to Lucien. And so he had. Just like that.

When Mara announced her engagement days after Paul's, her mother said: *You were like this as a girl too, only ever hungry the moment your brother was feeding.*

(

Simon goes left instead of right. He is taking the long way around to Jean's. Not the highway with its scattered gas stations and motels, but the dirt road hovering above the coastline. She can see it in the impossible darkness of the woods flanking the road: everything that she must unlearn about him, must unlove about him. *I don't want this to end either*, he tells her. *It doesn't have to*, she says, but her conviction is already gone. He keeps driving, past the turn to Jean's house, to the outskirts of the neighboring town, and further out; she doesn't dare ask where they are going. He doesn't say a word. He simply turns into a driveway, sighs his heavy sigh, and reverses course.

She is not sad, no. Gutted, yes. A clean cut down the middle and all the organs cupped, tossed off to the side.

⟨

On their way back to Jean's, Simon drives slowly, gripping the gearshift, his knuckles protruding, his hand seductively split into its individual fingers. She knows that for a moment, each had believed in it: that they might find it in each other, a clearing amidst the thicket. Beneath, the pine trees bowing their heads to the sin-dark sea, the fog slinking across the stubborn rocks. Straight ahead, the solidity of the yellow line, its unerring declaration: Do not cross me.

She could convince him, but what would be the point? A serpent eating its own tail, a game of hide-and-seek that refuses to end.

《

Jean's husband is the one who answers the door. He is wearing a white T-shirt, his belly a giant globe ready to pop. Mara's teeth are chattering, but she tries to get the words to sound like hers: *I'm a friend of Jean's. My car broke down nearby. I need a place to sleep, just for tonight.* His face is a series of ridges and ripples, the eyes deeply set in their sockets. *Well, that's not happening here. Jean could make friends with a kettle, so that doesn't mean a thing to me either, and I don't know what you've taken*, he grumbles, going off into the house. When she turns around, Simon's car is already gone.

She wakes before dawn, in a child's bed in a child's room. It takes her a moment to piece it together: this is the dead boy's room, the dead boy's bed. She remembers the night before: Simon, just a figure in a dream in which every single object is somehow estranged, misplaced, bizarre. To hope is to lose, she thinks. Simon didn't even wait until she was safely indoors. She had to ring Jean's doorbell again, beg. She follows the stars stuck on the ceiling with their dull, greenish hue, a wall of glossy photographs: tanned boys on surfboards dwarfed by giant waves. She gets up slowly, wades through the new status quo, looking for something familiar, a dock to hold onto, a moment to catch up to the new torrent of fact. In the mirror, a face, hers, but lined and puffy, mangled from the night before. No help there. Her face has always been this way: volatile, one way and then, without warning, another. In every photograph ever taken of her, she looks like a new version of herself, infinite variations on the same theme. Her sister-in-law looks the same in every photograph, a cutout from a magazine stuck into every important scene.

She moves slowly down the carpeted stairs. It's a modest, musty house. Everything in its spot, a form in which time has been pressed permanently into place. In the sink, a large casserole dish is waiting to be cleaned. She rolls her sleeves up, grabs at the wet mush of macaroni caked and softened down the sides. She scrubs, stopping from time to time to pick the starch off the metal bristles. She opens the ancient dishwasher, welcomes its mildewy smell: her mother's home when she could still manage it, her manic domesticity. She tries as best she can to put the dishes back on the correct shelves. She opens the cabinets slowly so they do not creak, makes the coffee, can't stand even the quiet rumble of the machine. She misses everyone, all at once. Or perhaps there is a missing so deep it has no single object, just a subject drowned out in the endless distance. She opens the pantry, finds the pancake mix, cracks an egg into a bowl and whisks it with some milk. Then the chocolate chips, dropped one by one, dark blots bobbing in a beige sea. She grabs the wooden spoon from the drawer, stirs. The batter sticks, resists her.

How did you think this would end? she'd spat at Lucien that last night. Of course, it was the worst kind of betrayal, to suggest that even her hope had been a lie, even her belief had been falsified. *I never thought that it would*, he told her, in a timbre so low, it struck her that he'd invented, in his sorrow, an entirely new key.

❨

Jean's husband is diabetic; he refuses the pancakes, sits with his arms across his chest, protesting her presence, her woman's unpredictability, his wife's complicity in this new setup. Jean is in a good mood. She enjoys the company; she talks in her easy way about town news, family members she saw and did not see over Christmas. *What a jerk*, she says of Simon. *Can't see a foot ahead of his own dick.* Even though Mara hasn't shared a thing about him, Jean's already guessed, as if no story could ever surprise her. Every person Jean describes has a fatal flaw, a single predicament without which their lives would be perfect. *She can't stay here, you know, in his room, I won't have it*, the husband interrupts, just as Jean is describing the rare strain of colon cancer eating her cousin up from within. Jean puts her finger to her lips and makes a loud shushing sound. *I didn't ask you, hun. Stay in your lane, would you?*

In the evening, Mara sits between them on the couch, overgrown teenager, biting at the fleshy half-moons of her fingernails. *Sometimes you have to turn the water off right at the main*, Lucien used to say. But now she can't remember in what context he used to say it.

《

She doesn't dare ask for a drink, and now in bed she can't think of anything else; every muscle in her face is gripped around it, this want: a violent spasm, a twitch. She'll wait until the TV is off and find the liquor cabinet. But they watch for hours, an entire lifetime spent in front of the blaring screen. She bites the inside of her cheek, pushes past the softness until she tastes the salty certainty. Hours go by; she cannot sleep. Her own sleep, her own life, she thinks, are like a team sport from which she has been permanently excluded. Finally, the television is off. Downstairs, she takes three gulps of the cinnamon-flavored whiskey she spotted earlier that evening on the kitchen counter. She nearly gags, and then just as quickly it comes over her: not happiness, not even relief, just the smallest breeze inside the cloistered room of her skin.

She could leave, of course. Find another town, maybe a city this time.

❮

Lucien used to say it to her all the time: *You'll do what you do either way, my love.*

She makes Jean and her husband a proposition: she can pay them money for the small room. *A thousand dollars a month!* Jean's husband blurts out, spooning clumps of oatmeal into his mouth. *Don't be an idiot*, Jean tells him. *This isn't San Francisco, for crying out loud. How about four hundred dollars?* The husband opens his mouth and then closes it again. *Shut it*, Jean tells him, just to make sure.

《

She finds, amidst a pile of the dead boy's neatly folded clothes, a thin fleece that fits. It smells sharp, recently washed. She can wear it under her hoodie until the weather warms. Charlotte's coat and boots and scarves she tucks away on the closet's farthest shelf. She retrieves her dirty white espadrilles, flattened at the bottom of her pack, patches them up with duct tape borrowed from the toolbox downstairs. When she is done, she brings them up to her nose, breathes in their familiar odor: damp rubber and rot.

Simon is standing by the door when she arrives at the shop on Monday morning. *I'm so glad that you came*, he tells her, his voice unnaturally strained. *I wasn't sure that you would.* She smiles at him: *It's my job. And you didn't tell me not to.* He comes closer: *Please, Mara.* But she moves out of his way and starts on her tasks. *As far as I'm concerned, what happened never happened, and now we're back at the beginning. You must be happy, you got what you wanted*, she tells him. He nods, his eyes bulging sadly. She is speaking a different language; he is a hapless tourist in the land of feeling.

(

She spends the day as if watching herself from a great height, a promontory above the city. She points from time to time, reminds herself: *This, here, is reality.* She welcomes each new customer with a warm smile. She makes one laugh and then another; she is in good form, moving around the store with the ease of the accustomed, the worn-in. Simon looks on at her, perplexed, nearly hurt, and then back down at his clipboard. He is taking dutiful inventory, preparing for an inspection, a surprise visit.

The day is done and there are only two options: the child's room in the strangers' home or the lonely stool at the town's only bar. And so, after Simon has locked up, she hangs back, then moves behind him, the back of his head a dark blot in the dim evening light. He was in her bed, just three days before, declaring: *I think I love you, Mara Tremblay.* If he looks back, she decides, then this is a sign, an omen, a promise that not everything has been lost. But he does no such thing. He walks with brusque determination away from the store, down Main and up to Summit. Of course, she was just a waypoint on the road home, the only open liquor store in a tiny town. When he reaches the top of the steep street, he pauses. This is it, she thinks. She waits for him to turn around, to remember, to come back to his senses, but he merely continues on his way, turning onto his street. She follows behind him. She stands nearby, not quite hidden by a tree. Once at the door, he feels around his pant pocket, and then the other, stands and waits before ringing the doorbell, a guest asking for permission to enter his own home. The door opens slowly and a queenly presence emerges: ginger locks piled atop her head and some majestic freckles across her nose and chest, a dark shawl slung self-regardingly around her shoulders. Mara sees it then, his shoulders slumped, his devotion, his wife's disregard for that devotion, the queen nodding in the direction of the road, the tree.

Mara does as children do. She closes her eyes: if she can't see them, then they can't see her. She waits for a long time this way. When she opens her eyes again, they are gone, the red door is in their place—stern, foreboding—a clenched fist hanging halfway up, a single glass eye staring her down.

❮

She's nobody, just a girl I hired to help around the store. That's what he'll say. She pictures them at the kitchen table, discussing what Charlotte missed while she was away. *Nobody*, a pile of dust swept into the shop's heating grate.

A week goes by. She waits for Charlotte to stop by the store. She looks to Simon for signs, but he is back to being inscrutable. He doesn't know what to do with her, so he does nothing at all. He moves his hand through his hair. Twirls his wedding band. He asks her how she is, and she says, *Fine*, and he answers, *Good, very good.*

«

Julian comes in when Simon is in the basement. *I heard*, he whispers, and takes her hand in his. She feels it now, in his sympathy, the sorrow she's been pushing under, a head bobbing up above the water. *I'm okay*, she says, *I just forgot myself, that's all.* She is holding him now, and she is weeping into his shoulder. *What are you going to do now, my dear?*

She sees them on Main Street, one early morning, Simon's wife and daughter, making their way into the pharmacy. They have the aura of celebrity, their coats and hats bright against the snow-streaked street. The girl is tall for a three-year-old and she holds her head a little like her mother, not looking around, strangely self-sufficient for a child. She has Simon's dark eyes and hair.

《

Mara moves behind them into the tiny pharmacy; she does not think. The pharmacist says hello, and Simon's wife turns around, smiles at Mara, a trace of something, a split-second lingering, and then she faces the counter again. It's just the smallest bit of eczema at the crook of the arm, she explains. She doesn't even know if she would call it eczema, but they've been in a warm climate and now suddenly back here in this damp cold again. *A warm climate*, not the name of a place, out of modesty perhaps, or because she is the kind of person who speaks from inside the closed loop of her own reference points. The little girl turns and Mara can't help but look at her, Simon's girl. The child does as children do, she simply stares back, unabashedly, until her mother picks her up, lifts up her sleeve to show the man behind the counter exactly where the rash has bloomed.

In the shop that day, she and Simon glide by one another without so much as a word. Simon is very good at this: turning the page, not flipping back to reread passages he enjoyed or misunderstood.

«

Charlotte shows up at the store a few days later, entirely unannounced. Her sense of ownership is palpably intact. *Such a pleasure*, she says, taking Mara's hand in hers, her voice thick with manufactured empathy: *I don't want to take up any of your time. I've just heard so much about you.* She's been meaning to come introduce herself, but she's been so busy since her return, cleaning up all the little messes. *You know the kinds I mean. Amazing what a year away can do to a place*, she says, looking around the store, suspicion flitting across her freckled face. Up close, the entire effect of her is diminished. Just the disparate parts vying for attention: the lines around her mouth and eyes, the uneven smattering of freckles across her cheeks and forehead, the halo of blond hairs bathing her face in an unseemly light.

When Simon comes back to the shop floor, she tells him: *Your wife stopped by just to say hi.* He looks flushed, despondent. *Oh right. She didn't want to stay? Did she say what it was about? Well, thanks, anyway, I hope that wasn't too strange for you.*

«

Every evening, after her shift is done, she climbs up the slick staircase, unseen, sits on the bare mattress until she is so cold and worn, she barely has the energy to get up and leave. She has never been very good at turning the page.

The next time Charlotte makes an appearance, she brings her daughter with her. Under the little girl's puffy snow-suit, she's been dressed up in pretty nautical stripes and a red headband, which she keeps tugging down, Charlotte pushing it back up with parental efficiency. *Mara, this is Ella*, Charlotte says, looking down at her daughter. *I hope this isn't a bother. I should be back in two hours*, as if every conversation were a fait accompli. Charlotte is out the door before there is time to protest, and there she is: the little girl, stranded in the middle of the shop floor, her bright eyes, the loose look of her arms by her sides. *You're the lady from the pharmacy, the one who was staring at me.*

Simon shows up just in time and, seeing his daughter standing there, declares in an aggrieved voice: *I don't understand why she asks me, if in the end she does exactly what she wants*, addressing neither Ella nor Mara. He lifts his daughter up, places her on his hip and walks around the shop, showing her what he thinks she may like: a bar of chocolate wrapped in gold paper and a paisley bow, the pastel sheen of the Jordan almonds in their crinkly pouch. He opens and closes the door to display the bell's mechanism. But he is doing it to occupy himself, to take his mind off things; Ella's attention is otherwise engaged. Her head swivels to find Mara wherever she is in the store. It is an effect Mara has had on children before: her deficiencies a source of endless interest. The phone rings, and suddenly the small body has been placed in her arms, warm and fragrant and wriggling, mouth open, heavy breathing, the staticky puff of hair billowing above her.

What's inside here? Mara says, sitting on the floor now, pointing to the girl's tiny plasticized backpack. Ella shrugs and scrunches her nose. *A banana?* Mara asks, shaking the bag a little. *No!* the little girl cries out. *An elephant?* she asks. *No!* squealing with delight. *A television?* Burbling laughter, which makes her belly tremble. *I know what it is . . .* Mara feels the contours of the bag and declares: *A vacuum cleaner!* They go on like this for a very long time, and when Mara is certain Ella is getting bored, Ella says, *Again!* and laughs, preempting her own pleasure. At some point, the child moves toward Mara's crouching leg and sits on it, as if Mara were a chair. She is heavier than she appears and the position uncomfortable, but Mara lays her hand around the soft belly, the child's body rising and falling with her breath, her hair just at nose height, sweet and matted from her winter hat, a swirl of dark fuzz at the back of her neck. Ella turns around, looks into Mara's eyes. *You're cute*, she declares, before pressing her wet nose against Mara's. Dizziness from the contact, the childish smell. When Simon comes to take her from her lap, Mara clings a moment longer than she should, until she feels the fat little limbs wriggling out from under her. *Thank you*, Simon mouths. *No problem*, she responds.

That night, she doesn't go upstairs, she goes straight to Jean's instead. Over her dinner of spaghetti with grated cheddar, she misses her—Ella—her animal warmth, the ease with which she climbed onto her lap, a trust so quickly granted, all the imagined stuff they'd fit, together, into her tiny backpack.

(

She counts backward: she is eight days late. She sweeps the thought away. *This* cannot be *that*.

On Sunday, she walks by their house. She sees Ella right away, standing on the soft couch, looking out onto the street. They lock eyes and the little girl smiles, waves jubilantly. She yells into the house, delighted, but just as quickly, Mara is off, fast enough, she hopes, so that Simon and Charlotte will think that their daughter has simply conjured the figure on the road in her mind.

On Monday, Charlotte descends on the store, worm squirming in her beak. *Simon is home sick with a cold*, she announces, nearly pleased. She is dressed for the job: hair up in a tight ponytail, thick-rimmed glasses, pencil neatly dug into the thick copper sheen of her hair. No mention of Mara's visit to the house. With Charlotte around, there is no time to think of what's past. Charlotte thinks only about the future, task upon task, every hour a building erected from scratch, brick by brick. She is the direct inheritor of the Protestant work ethic. *Onwards!* she says every time there is a dip in productivity. From time to time, Mara notices Charlotte watching her. She is coach and captain and referee, calculating where every player must stand on her field. Mara tries to work as she always does. She undresses the olives, cuts up some samples of cooked ham and a nutty sheep's cheese from the southwest of France. She begins to make the sandwiches. *You're cutting the baguette now?* Charlotte asks, hovering near her. *Simon thinks sandwiches grow on trees. We'll make them as we go along. It's dead here. I've seen it on the books, our worst season yet, so we have to be vigilant*, she says, grabbing Mara's shoulder meaningfully. Old friends. Sisters. *I work quite differently from Simon, but you'll see, we'll get along!*

Charlotte is the opposite of a coincidence. Everything she does is assessed, plotted. In her company, Mara feels useless, a jellyfish clinging to itself, the body a mere emanation of some distant nervous system.

((

In the new regime, Charlotte plays a compilation of world music and leaves the door wide open, despite the cold. *More inviting, non?* she declares. From time to time a draft reaches Mara and she shivers loudly. *We'll have to get you a warmer sweater, that one won't do!* Charlotte says, looking down at the linen one she has on, thin and inconsequential against her skin.

Mara disinfects the mop. She restocks the shelves. She slices the prosciutto. She seals and weighs it and prices it out. Charlotte inspects the work with godlike omniscience. If she is displeased, she doesn't say.

(

Mara takes the long way back to Jean's that evening. She cannot stand the look of the smug houses, their clapboard familiarity. She walks down through the thawing coastal brush, sliding across the wet rocks. The sea is dark, churning, spuming, pulling violently back out. *Stop*, she wants to tell it, *enough!*

The sun sets, the sky, a well-lit stage, then a curtain pulled down too fast. The only visible sign of life: a sliver of moon, butcher's hook looking to grab at tender flesh. She is that sliver, she thinks, slim and threatening, glinting in the night.

(

Lucien's ex-wife came to see her at the restaurant once. She didn't mince words. Lucien wanted children at all costs, she told Mara. And she hadn't been able to give him that. Mara could at least do that, couldn't she? A regret swaddled in a threat. From the moment they were married, Mara knew with a certainty she could only identify as fate: *I will fuck this up.*

A beach parking lot appears, emptied out, then further out, a long stretch of asphalt. She is further adrift than she thought, *Six Miles from Rome*, a sign spells out. She walks slowly, waiting for a honk, a flash of blinding light, but there is no one, nothing, just the sound of her own feet sloshing in her socks.

(

To think she used to dream of this place, or a town just like it, just like the one where her mother was born: picture-perfect in summer, bleak as death in winter.

Back at Jean's, she puts on a pair of clean socks, eats four rice crackers with orange cheese, and goes straight to sleep.

❨

In the dream, she is on a zipline, swinging back and forth across a gorge. On each end, a set of hands on her back, pushing her swiftly to the other side. At first, she thinks: What fun, to be so free, suspended amidst the trees. But she grows tired, dizzy from the endless back-and-forth. She yells out to stop, she needs to rest, but the hands are mindless, they do what they do without pause. The only solution, she figures, when she is halfway across, is to drop straight down onto the rocks.

In the shop the next day, Charlotte is in perfect form, carrying a fresh batch of bread pudding that Simon has made for the store. *Simon can be such a love*, she says, to no one in particular.

«

When she hears Simon's name in Charlotte's mouth, she has the petty thought: I know something you don't know. If Charlotte asked her what it was, this something, then she would say: *Nothing*, a thing known and then immediately lost. She was here when Charlotte was not.

She feels it all day, the frame tightening, the aperture closing.

❨

A feeling is a decision you get to make, Lucien used to like to say.

All day, she thinks: if she must go, then she will. All day, she thinks: there is nothing here for her anyway. But she doesn't know another place but this one anymore.

I'm tired of standing around, Charlotte declares, an hour before closing. *Choose a bottle, would you?* She smiles as if they are the oldest of friends, as if this newfound complicity must and will be shared. Charlotte moves easily around the shop. She brings back to the cafe table: a long piece of butcher paper dotted with a mound of carpaccio, chili-flecked olives, an oozing triple cream, and some rosemary crackers. Mara presents her with a Montepulciano, one of Simon's favorites. Charlotte pours two full glasses and without smelling hers, takes a disinterested gulp. The wine is heady: blackberries bursting in the crushing sun, opposite to the bleak exterior. *It's a bit much, isn't it?* Charlotte scrunches her nose. *Full of itself*, she says, looking up at Mara. She takes a cracker and uses it to spoon the gooey center of the triple cream. Her mouth is a little lazy; it refuses to close all the way. It's an alluring inconsistency, a flaw to settle into. *Might be time to freshen the place up, yes?* she says, taking a rolled-up piece of junk mail and using it to point at various cracks in the ceiling, a fissure creeping up along the back wall. *I'll have to talk to Dad about it, of course. He holds the purse strings around here. He's very generous, though, always has been.* She drinks quickly; she is immediately sharper and also looser somehow. *You look surprised. Simon didn't tell you, of course. He's so fixated on appearing righteous. It's so childish, really.*

Charlotte takes another swallow, tightens her eyes into feline slits. *I've been meaning to thank you. You look surprised. Don't be. You're very special to us, you know, Mara.* Charlotte rests her hand on Mara's forearm. *I want to be very honest here. Simon told me about you. It must have been a few weeks ago. On the phone. Mara this, Mara that. I was in the Yucatán, of all places, and yet, it made an impression! At first, of course, I didn't like it. I think I was a little jealous. But then, in the end, it's what got me to come back, to make the decision. And so I started to think that maybe it had been a bit of a ploy all along. Simon's not as guileless as he seems. Nothing against you, of course, but I know Simon better than he knows himself. He would have done anything to get us back.*

(

She pictures it: she the worm squirming at the tip of Simon's fishhook.

She should be angry, insulted even, but she sees it, coursing beneath Charlotte's cruelty: her terror.

（

Mara stands up, takes her glass to the sink and rinses it once, twice, three times, takes her leave. Enough is enough is enough.

Back at home, Jean says: *You look like you got hit by a truck.*
Her husband is gone and she's drinking a pint glass of boxed
chardonnay. *Sit*, she says, pointing to the drooping armchair.
Mara lays back, lets Jean rake her fingers through her hair.
Your scalp is so tight, she says. *What's on your mind, girl?*
She shakes her head. *Nada*, she says, closes her eyes again.

((

In the dead boy's room, she dreams of everyone: Simon
and Charlotte and Ella, Paul and his wife, her mother, her
mother-in-law, old friends and boyfriends, acquaintances
from restaurants where she used to work, years ago now.
Even her father appears; she hasn't seen him in over ten
years. But not Lucien. She never dreams of Lucien anymore. She heard once that every person in every dream is
in fact a version of you. Maybe Lucien, then, is the only
one who has loosened himself from her mind's hold, from
the self's grip. Not a symbol, not a fun-house distortion,
just Lucien: plain and simple. The beginning of a new set
of metaphors and meanings she simply refused, in the end,
to give herself over to.

She inspects her sheets, her underwear; it should have come by now.

(

When Jean and her husband have left for the day, she makes her way down the stairs, slinks around the house, a babysitter on the prowl after her wards have gone to bed. She should be at work by now. She opens and closes drawers, puts on Jean's terry-cloth robe, circles the paisley bedspread in their room, opens a photo album, spreads it out on the peach floor. The same blond boy in every photograph, a baby, a child, a teenager now, laughing in every single still. She can nearly see it, etched in that smile, his fate.

In the kitchen cupboard, she finds the instant coffee and heats the milk up on the stovetop, adds three teaspoons of sugar and stirs until the milk is nearly hissing, it's so hot. She pours it into a cup, takes one sip, swallows back a sob.

❨

Nada, she thinks. If it's a girl.

She takes her mug to the back patio, sits on the wet steps, stares out. But she is quickly bored, moves, in her flimsy espadrilles and oversized bathrobe, across the dull, wet grass. She finds a gap among the branches and makes her way into the barren woods. The last of the snow sits in stubborn pine-needled lumps. She skips from rock to root on her tiptoes, circumnavigating the wet spots. But within moments, she trips, and both her espadrilles are slick with mud. Another step and the cold slime makes its way over the lip of her ankle socks. She barely feels the cold, though; she is so glad to be back afoot, out of doors. She follows her breath, a plume of spring in the bower's wintry mouth. Tender heads of bracken fronds, shy in their unfurling. She wonders if she will stay here long enough to see them in their full expression, their deferent bowing. She reaches a steep incline, and instead of turning back, she ties Jean's bathrobe tighter around her waist, gets down on her knees, claws her way up.

At the top of the steep hill, a clearing. Beneath her, the thicket of pines, a smattering of houses flattened by perspective, the blushing frenzy of blueberry bushes clustered around a bog. Between two trees, she thinks she can make it out, the sea, that tyrant. She lifts her thumb up to nose-height, covers up the spot.

(

She composes, in her head, the letter she will write to Charlotte, describing every whispered touch, every last word, every withheld breath. *Your husband and I* will be the opening phrase of every paragraph, she decides. How easy: a phrase like a grate lifted and then, just the softest tap, the burning log rolled out into the middle of their living room floor.

She shouldn't, but she does it anyway, turns right instead of left. *When there's a fork in the road, take it.* Lucien's pleasure at his own worn-out jokes. When she arrives at their house, she sees him through the window, Simon, his familiar profile, bathing in the TV's anesthetic glow. Charlotte, she knows, will still be at the store. She rings the bell and it takes him a while to come. But when he opens the door, and he is there before her, she understands: nothing is ever over; you can never really unknow; there is no such thing as recovery, no such luxury as forgetting. *Mara? What's wrong? Why are you dressed that way? Did something happen? Is Charlotte okay?* His automatic response, his mind's singular track. She wants to take her hand to his hair, push the wild strands to one side. She touches her own hair instead. She doesn't know what she's come to say. I missed my period, Simon. Love *me* instead.

You're not sick, then, she tells him once they are inside, in the kitchen, in this home he's never let her visit. She has taken off her shoes and socks; her feet are blackened, the toenails caked with dirt. *No*, he says, looking right through her. *Not really. I just needed a change of pace. To be away from the store for a while. To spend some time with my daughter. It's in everyone's best interest, we think.* She can see him so plainly now: ventriloquist for Charlotte's every wish. *And Charlotte has very much enjoyed working with you. Don't look at me like that, Mara, it's true. You look awful. I'm worried about you*, he tells her, putting his hand on her shoulder.

❦

Don't, she says, pulling away. She asks to use the bathroom. *Upstairs to the left*, he tells her, pointing to the stairway. *But quickly, Mara. Charlotte will be here any minute and she can't see you like this.* In the full-length mirror in the vestibule, she sees what she has done: nose runny, hair thistled, arms crisscrossed with cuts, kneecaps scraped clean.

SARA FREEMAN

She retches into the toilet but nothing comes out. If she tells him, he'll feel obliged to her, that much she knows. A single tug and she'll unravel the entire tapestry of his life. A noise from a nearby room, the rustling of sheets and a low whine. She moves toward it, and there she is, Ella, sleeping in her little room. She is squirming in her sheets, in the midst of a bad dream. Mara moves in next to her, *It's me, Mara. I'm here.* Ella mumbles, sits up, opens her eyes and then lies back down, still asleep. Mara touches the damp forehead, pushes the strands back behind her ears. *There, there, it was just a bad dream.* Ella rolls over, her body facing Mara's lap. *Your sister's in here now,* Mara whispers, laying Ella's hand on her belly. But the little one is fast asleep, takes her arms instinctively back to her sides. Suddenly a wave of exhaustion; Mara will lie down for just a moment. She closes her eyes, lays her arm over the sleeping mound beside her.

❨

She refused to hold the child in the end. She let Lucien take her in his arms, let Lucien deal with it all.

She wakes, Simon and Charlotte shining down on her, their faces distorted, pulling at her arms, dragging her out of the small bed. Ella opens and closes her eyes, squirms, moans. *You're sick. You're really sick, did you know that?* Charlotte says, walking Mara down the stairs, Simon stiffened in his tracks. *I'll call Jean to give you a ride, Mara*, he says, in a whisper. Charlotte opens the door, pushes her out into the balmy evening air. *You can wait outside, then get out of our lives*, she declares before slamming the door.

((

Ours, that was her sister-in-law's favorite word.

In the car, Jean is furious. *I don't know what you did, but you don't deserve to be put to the curb like that, that's for sure.* At the stoplight, she looks over at Mara. *I, for one, am glad you're here. You've done me a world of good. We'll get you cleaned up and good as new and if you need work, I've got a few leads. You know me. I know every guy in this town.* Mara nods soundlessly. When they hit a pothole, she reaches reflexively for her belly.

(

When she'd first heard she was pregnant, it was his face that she pictured—Paul's—the way he was as a little boy. And then she'd gotten the news: not a boy but a girl. The thought had emerged, unbidden, announcing its miserable news: she didn't want that at all.

Back in the house, she sits in the bathtub, watches the water turn gray. It is nowhere near bedtime, but inside her bedroom, she closes the curtains and pretends. They used to do this as children, she and Paul, when they were bored witless. They would lie down in their mother's bed and close their eyes, for just as long as they could bear it. When they opened their eyes again, Mara would yawn, ask Paul to tell her what he'd dreamed. But he never could come up with a good one on the spot. He was weighed down by the details, by his devotion to reality. It was Mara who was expert at the game, who wanted to find an image so apt, their entire lives might glide like damp thread through the eye of the needle.

❨

Her first word, allegedly, was *mine*. Paul's was *Mara*, although their mother would insist, later, that it was *Mama*.

She sleeps and wakes, sleeps again. In the dream, she is strapped to the hull of a very tall ship. She will go wherever it takes her, she will take whatever blow comes her way.

❨

Sometimes she wonders what might have happened if she'd been born less flawed, if she'd turned, on occasion, right instead of left. Maybe then she'd be more like Paul, not a bay stripped bare by the tides, all the scum and rocks and dented plastic bottles on hideous display.

She wakes, clutching her stomach. No time has passed;
Lucien is by her side. He touches her stomach with his palm.
Nearly there, he says, speaking sweetly into her bellybutton.

(

She sensed it, of course, two months before she was due.
A silence where there was once a hum. Cold stone in her
shoe. She told no one. She spent nine days this way, lead-
weighted, a tomb. Until she felt the first of her contractions,
bitter relief, the body giving birth to what was already dead:
her pulseless creature, her will-less form.

She was blameless. Who said that? A doctor. And then another after that. Her sister-in-law even piped up. *You did nothing wrong*, she confirmed, for the first time since she had known her. Only Mara knew the truth—her guilt a loose tooth at the back of her mouth that only she could touch.

☾

And then an absence, a blank space where life had nearly taken hold.

He was born, theirs, her brother's and his wife's, only days after hers was born dead. She held him and she knew right away. She never said it out loud, of course. She didn't make that mistake. *Mine*: she knew how that would sound. Unhinged, deranged. She felt it anyway, in no small way, that the child was hers.

A knock at the door, a benevolent presence above her. *You were yelling*, Jean whispers. She sits, places Mara's head on her soft lap, touches her moist forehead. Jean's body smells of mulch, and pine, and something sharper, bleach or maybe vodka. Mara can feel Jean's hand moving down, resting knowingly on her chest. *Your heart is beating so fast*, Jean says. The hand moves lower still, onto her breast now, a smooth maternal touch, decisive. A palm on her bare skin. *There, there.* She is asleep, but she can hear Jean now, her hand working under her, touching herself, *there, there,* the voice says, breath quickening. Mara doesn't mind; she feels calm amidst someone else's pleasure. A wave slapping up against a stone wall. Then the soft release, the wet heat, like holding a shell up to her ear. *I'm sorry, Mara, I don't know what came over me, go back to sleep.* She is whispering now, stroking Mara's hair, *there, there.*

How easy it was, as in a dream, not a single decision to make. She only had to undo one button, and there he was, his warm face nosing against her skin, her breasts bruised peaches, soft and tender beneath him. She moved the dark nipple into his mouth. He took it between his little lips, colder than she'd thought they'd be, the gums hard against the flesh. First he didn't latch. Babies know their mothers, after all. Then he suckled but nothing came, until she felt it, the throb, the sudden surge of milk from her weeping breast into the newborn's hungry mouth. An immeasurable calm washed over her. Everything wrong suddenly made right.

She knows it is morning, but she can't get herself to open her eyes, to greet the light, the decisions that must be made. She wants to wade in it longer, swim out a little farther.

☾

He walked in on her, not the first time but the third, Paul. His baby feeding, legs kicking happily beneath. He said nothing at first, just took his boy out of her arms. She didn't try to apologize or explain. *You couldn't help yourself, could you?* he said. In his face as known to her as her own, she could see, reflected, her suspicion finally finding its ugliest form: how wrong she'd become. *I won't tell them*, he said quietly. She heard then what it might do to him in the end, this endless collusion between them, his sweet humming along to her tune. He'd always been this way, a perfect shadow, loyal to a fault.

For days after the incident, she would wake up having forgotten that any of it had taken place. And even when she remembered, it was a kind of forgetting, a blank screen nested in a blank screen nested in another blank screen, her mind a vacated mise-en-abîme.

《

There's something very wrong with Mara. Everyone said that.

Her mother called to warn her that if she didn't get her act together, Lucien would leave her. *Pity is not an aphrodisiac, remember that*, she said, lending out, in her version of a charitable act, this pearl of regret.

❝

You are me and I am you. It was a trick her mother must have taught them how to play.

But Lucien wanted to start over. *We can try again*, he told her, dog with his own bone. She was the one who forced him to go. She was the one who couldn't bear the weight of all his stubborn hope.

❨

When I was pregnant, I slept with a man on the dirty floor of a cocktail bar and then another after that. I took two shots of vodka every night before bed. I dreamed every night that our child would die. And then her grand finale, cherry on top, sucker punch, her only lie: *I don't love you anymore.* Anything to get him to finally say, *Enough!*

She walked all the time in those days, to the edge of the city where the sidewalk stopped, and then back again. She could think of only one thing then: a town by the sea. A place like the one where her mother was from. She must have wanted to rewind, to return to a time before she was born, before everything was set in motion, in stone.

《

Alone in the house, she takes a shower, puts on the cleanest clothes she can find. She should leave, find another town, maybe a city this time.

Outside, the sun is high and bright; white rot mottling the lawn. This is the ugliest season, she decides, everything sodden before it revives. She wants to see the town one last time before she goes.

❨

The town sign reads: *This Road Leads to Rome*, with an ugly drawing of the Colosseum, followed by the population, 2,353.

On Main Street, everything is as it has always been: serene, unyielding. She sees the town hall first, its understated conceit, walks past the shop window. Inside she can make out: Charlotte standing behind the cheese counter, pencil in her hair, the infuriating curve of her spine, chest pressed out like a shield. Simon is seated on an upside-down crate, fiddling with a screwdriver. They look like what they are: a husband and a wife. She walks past them, senses them disappearing into her blind spot.

All the way to the end of Main Street, past the clothing store and the laundromat, and the still-closed ice cream shop, past the public beach and further still to the hostel's lot. It was an armory before, with its thick, rounded walls. It is only March; no efforts have been made to open it up for the season. She finds the window on the second floor, the one in her first room, and then the other, a single porthole at the far end of the dormitory, the one she shared with the men. She could wait until their return, stay for the summer months, make her decision then.

When she pictures it—herself in this town forever—it reminds her of a silent movie she once saw in which a man, shot dead on a sidewalk, steps out of the outline the police chalked, looks down at his own figure, then, satisfied with the line, settles back down, closes his eyes, dies all over again.

❨

Ça suffit, she mouths, following the yellow line out of town. Tightrope walk, gangplank. *Enough is enough is enough*, all the way back to Jean's pale, vinyl-sided house.

She saw them, right before she left, walking hand in hand on Saint-Denis, Lucien and his ex-wife. Every single thing that had happened between Mara and Lucien as verifiable as a forgotten dream. She ducked into a bedding store, rammed a fist into her mouth so she wouldn't cry out.

She packs her bag, unpacks it again, leaves everything she owns strewn on the floor. The split fountain pen, the stranger's ID, the addict's ragged sweatshirt, Charlotte's winter clothes, library books stacked high. All her pilfered stock. She doesn't know what she's waiting for. A sign, a kick at the door. Someone to tell her that she must go. Someone to tell her to come home. She touches the old cell phone, turns it on its side, pulls it apart, blows into every sandy slot, replaces the parts. She holds the button down until the screen blinks then sings back to life. A ping, a message welcoming her to the United States, and then another and another, a neighborly onslaught. Paul's name flashes onto the screen. She wades through his messages, the eddies of his distress, his modest pleas trailing off in January. Then she moves to those from friends and colleagues, a small flurry of concern. Not a word from Lucien. She lets the finality of that fact reach her. Her hands shake as she rereads her brother's final missive: *We just want to know you're alive, Mar.* Not a single mention of her coming home. She cries softly, then more loudly, her resolve thickening as she types: *I'm alive, Paul. You don't need to worry about me anymore.* Then her voicemails assault the screen. Most are from her mother, at least a dozen of them. She takes her thumb to the side of the little machine, turns it off before that current claims her.

Lying in bed, it is all that she can hear, the sea on the other side of the state road, carrying her out and hauling her back in. She puts her pillow over her ear, tries to dampen the obstinate song.

(

She moves around the house after dark, when she knows she won't bump into her hosts. She gathers provisions, sneaks them back upstairs: a bowl of sugary cereal, a bag of marshmallows, a shot of whiskey she sloshes around and, to her surprise, spits back out into a cup.

She wakes early the next morning, bathed in the knowledge that only sleep yields. The thought, an elastic band held taut, snapped right back.

«

On y va, ma belle, she whispers, reaching down to the tender heat of her abdomen. *We're off, my love.*

It takes no time to pack up her clothes, to strip the bed, to tidy the tiny room. She's rehearsed this scene so many times before. Jean and her husband are downstairs, laughing, rare soundtrack in this house. From the bathroom cabinets she collects a roll of toilet paper, some aspirin, some multivitamins, two toothbrushes from a twelve-pack, stuffs them into her bag. She takes the boy's fleece off, folds it up, places it back in its spot. She leaves the library books in a neat stack on the floor, fits the biography of the famous chef back into her pack. She waits at the top of the stairs until she has heard the garage door clicking, the bandsaw running, his Sunday tinkering.

In the kitchen, Jean looks up shyly over her cup of coffee. She takes note of Mara's bag, the overstuffed totes. *You're leaving? This is all my fault. Forgive me!* She looks rosy, young even, years recovered in just a few days. Mara is glad she's served some purpose in this house, this town. *Not at all*, she says, hugging Jean goodbye. *Not at all.*

She jots her farewell note on one of the blank pages at the back of her book. She walks past Main, the closed-up shop, up to Summit and to the red door. No car in the driveway, no lights on. *I'm off. I'll be alright!* she writes. But that's not quite right. She takes the pen out, makes the necessary marks. She folds the note in two, writes *S&C* on the front flap, slips it through the slot.

Later she'll regret it, of course, crossing the *I*'s out, writing those *we*'s instead.

❨

All roads lead to Rome. She knows there is no such thing as a clean cut. And yet she can't help but feel it, growing inside her, something like hope.

She hitches a ride to the nearest city from a man driving a truck full of beanbags and plastic plants. At the gas station, he rolls the back door up and shows them to her: drooping balls and glistening ferns, plastic jungle, ersatz world, no mulch or rot. *Really makes you wonder*, he tells her, but she doesn't know about what.

On the long bus journey out from the city, she doesn't cry or even have a single thought that she can name. She watches the dark possibility of the road instead, the mostly empty seats ahead of her, the head of a man a few rows up, listing forward and then jolting back. She does not sleep. She wants to be awake so she can remember this moment later: neither a beginning nor an ending, but both. A woman across the aisle, after hours of silence between them, turns and asks, *Where to?*

ACKNOWLEDGMENTS

I would like to thank Caroline Beimford, Gabriella Lindsay, Lexi Freiman, Meara Sharma, Stacey D'Erasmo, Sanaë Lemoine, and Emma Cline for reading early drafts and providing wisdom and encouragement. Thank you to Marina Kasdaglis, for listening so well. Thank you to Bob Fox for introducing me to the repetition compulsion. Thank you to Anna Stein, my dream agent, and to Julie Flanagan and everyone at ICM who has helped this book find a home in the world. Thank you to my fantastic UK agent, Sophie Lambert, and to Meredith Ford at C&W. A special thank you to Elisabeth Schmitz, for all of her expertise and grace, and to Yvonne Cha and the rest of the wonderful team at Grove Atlantic. Thank you to Laura Barber at Granta Books, for her insight and dedication. Thank you to Deborah Sun De La Cruz at Hamish Hamilton Canada, for her sensitivity and attention to detail. A big thank you to my brother, Samuel Freeman, for reading and believing from the beginning. Thank you to my parents,

ACKNOWLEDGMENTS

Susan Côté-Freeman and Alan Freeman, for their loving support. Thank you to Annlee Landman, for sharing her cottage by the sea. Thank you to the entire Côté-Freeman-Tang-Landman clan, for making life richer. Thank you to the Bread Loaf Writers' Conference, for the time on the mountain. Thank you to my friends, for the company and the care. Thank you to my teachers and to my students, for the ongoing conversation. Lastly, thank you, Jeffrey Landman, for all you make possible.

The following essay by Sara Freeman
was first published in the *Big Issue*
on March 14, 2022.

In the summer of 2017, I left New York City, where I had been living for seven years, and moved to Boston, Massachusetts. My time in NYC had been mixed. I had tried and failed to get my first novel published; I had worked a job I found meaningful, but which offered no health insurance, no future. By the end of my stay, I was weary of the city, which reminded me, every day, of all I hadn't achieved by staying. And so I left, glad for the leaving.

And yet, once I settled in the new city, near the university where my husband would be attending architecture school, a new weariness crept in. On Saturday mornings, my husband long gone to the studio, I wandered the sleepy neighborhood, with its introverted students and purposeful joggers, and looked for a street life, a civic sense, any sign really of the life I might lead, now that I had left the old one behind.

An image often came to me then of the Italian cafe in Montreal I used to frequent in university, of that companionable time in my life before I knew I wanted to write. Or sometimes my mind wandered further afield and I let myself take a bus somewhere, anywhere, a town by the sea maybe. The town itself mattered less than the room where I would stay. In this room, I was always alone, with just what I needed: a single bed, a chair, a desk, an electric kettle, a pen and paper, and a door I could close and lock behind me.

I have always been drawn to books and movies that depict their characters, most often women, walking away from their lives: leaving their spouses, their children, their cities, their apartments, their jobs. Anne Tyler's *Ladder of Years* is one such work. It's a conventional story, about a forty-year-old middle-class Baltimore woman, Delia, who finds herself leaving her husband and three children while on a beach vacation. She hitches a ride to a nearby town, and slowly builds a life there that in its ascetism and solitude seems as far away, at least at first, from the old one as possible.

Alone for the first time in her life, Delia discovers her own desires, separate from her relationships, from the roles she's tacitly taken on—mother, wife, sister, secretary, lynchpin of her family's social and domestic lives. Each mundane object she acquires for her spartan boarding house room—a gooseneck lamp, an immersion water heater, a romance novel—is a triumph in the face of her history of compliance.

I must have wanted, my first year in the new city, that kind of solitude too, the kind one chooses in a single, decisive act of free will. Although I had been hopeful that the move might help me write another novel, I had left, in truth, not for myself but for my husband's degree. And as I tried to get up the nerve to start over, I was met with a familiar, disheartening feeling, that in leaving I had somehow become the one left behind.

In *Ladder of Years*, despite every effort to escape her domesticated, gendered experience, Delia ends up—in ways so subtle, so subconscious, in short, so true to life—recreating the very circumstances she so longed to escape. Our patterns, our relationships, our histories aren't so easy, the book suggests, to shake off.

Spring came, and I made a friend and then another. I volunteered at the local women's center. I met women there who had had no choice but to leave their cities, their homes, their families. They'd been evicted, displaced, exiled to the margins of society by exclusionary systems.

One woman rode the overnight bus back and forth from Boston to New York City for the cheap night's sleep, the other recounted the dreams she had of the daughter she'd not seen since she was a baby, and another talked of the French degree she'd loved but abandoned after too many devastating losses. Women's lives, it struck me, were always on a knife's edge between relationship and alienation, resilience and despair.

Around the same time, I found a library with a desk by a perfect window, suspended above the trees, overlooking an ancient cemetery and a church steeple, its clock being carefully refurbished. The nook had no door, no lock, and no kettle but it was a sliver large enough to fit my modest ambition: to try to write another novel, about a woman who leaves everything behind after a personal tragedy.

The women I'd come to know from the center, and those from the books and movies I loved, kept me company during those long months, and I discovered alongside them a permission to be alone in a new way, one I had never granted myself before. In writing my novel *Tides*, I found a kind of leaving that allowed me to stay in place, to be alone in the company of others.

Keep in touch with
Granta Books:

Visit granta.com to discover more.

GRANTA